LOUSE

DAVID GRAND

DAVID GRAND

LOUSE

ARCADE PUBLISHING • NEW YORK

The author wishes to acknowledge:

H. H., for living so strangely.

Alex Todorovic, for the correspondence that started this. Rachel Andrews, for much inspiration. Christopher Connelly, for reading and rereading each and every draft, and for always providing keen insight.

E. L. Doctorow, for helping me see the promise.

My editor, Sean McDonald, for taking so much care to make it what it is.

My agent, John Hodgman, for his fortitude, wit, and diligence.

My family: Margie and Joel, Adam and Staci, for all the encouragement along the way. The elders: Bessie and Harry, Lil and Seymour, for sticking around to see it published. And Christine, my beautiful wife, for the love and support this book needed to exist.

I am also grateful to Diane Gurman, Allan Hardy, Robert Ramirez, and Kathryn Sears.

FIRST EDITION

This is a work of fiction. Names, characters, places and incidents are either the product of the author's imagination or used fictitiously.

Library of Congress Cataloging-in-Publication Data

Grand, David, 1968–
    Louse / David Grand. —1st ed.
      p.   cm.
    ISBN 1-55970-449-7
    I. Title
  PS3557.R247L6 1998
  813'.54—DC21   98–20281

Published in the United States by Arcade Publishing, Inc., New York
Distributed by Little, Brown and Company

10 9 8 7 6 5 4 3 2 1

Designed by Sean McDonald

BP

PRINTED IN THE UNITED STATES OF AMERICA

For Christine

Boredom is the root of all evil, and it is this which must be kept at a distance. Idleness is not an evil, indeed one may say that every human being who lacks a sense for idleness proves that his consciousness has not yet been elevated to the humane.

KIERKEGAARD, EITHER/OR

And they said every one to his fellow, Come, and let us cast lots, that we may know for whose cause this evil is upon us.

BOOK OF JONAH 1:7

LOUSE

OM 33D: FILIN

MEMO 1.1.1.

TO: MR. HERMAN Q. LOUSE

As head of the Resort Town of G., I wish to welcome you. Though you will find your long-term memory impaired, you will find your short-term memory fully functional. Your motor skills should be impeccable and your energy level appropriately blissful, as well as suitable for all required duties and activities. Our facility is climate controlled, pressure sensitive, and fully alert. You will find your uniform (one gray flannel suit with matching vest, starched white shirt, blue tie, black socks, black wing tips) appropriately arranged in your closet. In your desk drawer, you will find one copy of your initial contract, signed, dated, and witnessed, along with one regulation fly swatter, one syringe, one bottle of appropriate pharmaceutical, and one handkerchief. Each of these items is to be replaced nightly as per Memo 3.3.3. (to be found on top of your desk beside this greeting). Moreover, you will find one pocket watch, one list of Federal Gaming Commission protocol, one pair of AA batteries, a three-foot tape measure, one pen to be kept in left inner breast pocket, and one bottle opener, which is to remain attached to your watch chain.

Congratulations on your indoctrination.

Your Devoted Guardian,
Herbert Horatio Blackwell
Executive Controlling Partner

(FOUND IN A SAFETY DEPOSIT BOX IN THE CITY OF N.)

EPOSIT BOX I

MEMO 3,333
TO: ALL WARDS OF THE RESORT TOWN OF G.

If all has gone according to plan, I will have taken my final flight over the valley this morning and one or more of you will have reached this final destination. Please find enclosed the names, addresses, and phone numbers of your next of kin, as well as account information regarding compensatory damages in the title of a trust, "Reparations for Herbert Horatio Blackwell's Injustices to Humanity," which is to be distributed monthly for the remainder of your natural lives.

You and your families will be well provided for, and I and other members of the Resort Town of G. will no longer be of concern to you, or them. For I, and whomever else you may possibly fear, will have been properly taken care of, harshly punished well beyond the full extent of the law.

You may not have the immediate satisfaction of seeing us publicly humiliated; however, once you have normalized your lives, you will have much time and many opportunities to vilify us in the worst possible light using the most sophisticated contemporary documentation methods known to man.

I leave it to you to make of it what you will. And the best of fortune to you!

Yours sincerely,
Herbert Horatio Blackwell
Executive Controlling Partner

Sometime in the present...

1. THE EXECUTIVE CONTROLLING PARTNER

TIVE CONTROL

Poppy's Valium Librium Empirin #4 fills the brim of an unblemished vial. His syringe, capped by a short plastic nipple, rests on a puff of white gauze. A flaccid rubber tube coils into the shape of a circular maze. All the items are meticulously arranged on a hospital tray whose stainless steel reflects the dim red glow of camera surveillance lights. My hands are suited with rubber gloves. My face is masked. My hair is shaved from my head and arms. I smell of a sweet coconut-scented antiseptic.

"The nights feel longer, Mr. Louse," Poppy says as he wakes from a deep sleep.

"Yes, sir."

"The days feel shorter."

"Yes, sir."

"Mr. Louse?"

"Yes, sir?"

"Which one is it?"

"It is night, Poppy."

"The nights feel longer."

"Yes, Poppy. They do."

Poppy breathes shallow breaths as I place his tray onto the corner of the western night table and bend over his body to search for a point of entry. As I hover over him, his forehead thickens into wrinkled folds of flesh. Within them, the folds contain clusters of what look like shattered pearls. The icy fissures cascade into tufts of a long auburn beard, greasy and patched with streaks of lint-gray. The slick hair languidly folds over his lips and jowls in such a manner that it's very difficult to read any form of expression on his face. If his beard should silently jostle around, I often imagine various affectations and looks, as, say, when one imagines life bustling about under the gaseous surface of a distant planet. I might perceive, for instance, phantoms of irony or bitterness or despair, a silent request whose message I feel individually responsible for.

Any kind of bodily motion shakes the few remaining hairs straddling his scalp; they shake and twist like antennae homing in on coded frequencies, always followed by his voice, his commands, which are delivered with a steady and stiff timbre. His eyes hide in the shadows of thick beetle-brows and high cheek bones. When they are visible, they are distant and shy, veiling his dictates with numb appraisals.

"Try here," he says, rolling over onto his stomach. With a looping brown finger nail, he points me down the shingled path of his body. My eyes travel the curves of the nail to his loin cloth. The elastic waist hugs the bones of his hips, which are distended and sharply angle into his legs. His skin is like moth-eaten velvet and shimmers like the phosphorescence of a crashed wave. I fear that a slip of the finger will puncture or bruise its cloudy sheen.

As I take hold of the back of his knee I begin humming the third movement of Mozart's "Requiem" in the key of D minor. I am to hum this as I search for a point of entry. Poppy's few remaining open veins appear and disappear and reappear. When I find a thin streak of blue that I think might take the needle, his tendons stiffen and his muscles contract. I uncoil the tube and tie it around his leg. Taut. Very taut. He likes to lose all sensation. He likes the rush that results when I release the tension. According to his last memo, I am to *constrict whichever part of [his] body [I have] to in order to find the most functional vein.*

The low moan of the chambers' ventilation system changes frequency as Poppy sighs from the back of his throat.

"Tighter, Mr. Louse."

"Yes, Poppy."

I tie the band tighter.

He coughs a little, and then, as instructed, I take hold of the syringe between my forefinger and middle finger. I remove the plastic nipple from the tip of the needle and place it on the tray. I push the plunger with my thumb, stick the needle in the vial, and pull the plunger back up. When the liquid fills to the proper measure, I tap away the remaining air bubbles inside the tube. I say, "I am ready, sir." He doesn't say anything in response. Confirmation that I am ready is all he requires.

I am to rest my left forefinger at the point of entry. I am to insert the needle slowly so that he feels it enter. I am then to insert it as deeply as it will go. I place my left forefinger over an open lesion and slowly and deeply insert.

His leg spasms a little.

He sighs again.

I push the plunger down, but only halfway. I am to push the plunger halfway, then I am to pull back. This works to mix his blood with the compound, which is heavy on codeine, light on aspirin, caffeine, phenacetin. I wait a moment longer. Then I push the new mixture into his vein. I remove the needle as slowly as I inserted it and delicately replace it on the tray. I remove the rubber band and recoil.

I stop humming.

Poppy's foot trails off to the edge of the bed. His chest falls into his pillows. He picks up on Mozart's melody from where I left off, humming a nasal hum.

I promptly step away from him toward a large picture window covered with long smooth sheets of aluminum foil. The window nearly runs the length of the western wall and has never revealed anything more than a dim reflection of Poppy's chambers—the bed, a nightstand, the television, and a sprawl of discarded newspapers, legal pads, and Kleenex that surrounds the bed's periphery.

I proceed around the sprawl of papers and under the low-lying ducts of the ventilation system. The ventilation system, which is heat sensitive, prevents mold and mildew from collecting on or within these papers' fibers, or between any ordinary crevices for that matter, in gaps of generally unseen and unimagined space. Poppy's chambers are so dry, in fact, that on occasion, a corner of an old *Wall Street Journal* has been known to curl up like the ear of a curious dog.

Over time, the debris deposited around Poppy's bed has shaped itself into small mounds resembling mountain ranges. Peaks and valleys, plateaus and plains, buttress against the edges of canyons and ravines made of uneven folds of newsprint. It is not hard to imagine that if water were to fall from the ceiling, creeks, streams, and rivers would flow into lakes and estuaries, and Poppy's bed would buoy up like a raft floating over the black-bottom silt of a swamp.

I close the door to his chambers so that it slams shut. This way he can hear the latch click and imagine my hand falling comfortably to my side. I bow my head, dim the lights of the long hallway, and walk with slow strides toward the kitchen.

The floors of the western wing, as well as the eastern, northern, and southern wings, are covered in gray linoleum. The red pulses of camera surveillance lights flicker and streak down the glossy finish. The illumination reflects off glass cabinets filled with Poppy's paper planes, of which there are thousands, each named for either Kathryn, Betty, or Jane, women whose holographic images adorn the medicine cabinets in the three bathrooms adjoining Poppy's chambers. Each woman looks down over her own province of scrubbed white marble. Each has eyes that can see to anywhere in her room. The heads turn as a subject crosses before them and nod when a subject kneels to the floor. The images, in their entirety, are equipped to glow in the dark; when they do, they cast a soft greenish hue onto the walls.

Kathryn is the youngest and most pouting of the three. Her hair is long and slightly drapes over her left cheek. Her eyes are round, but appear narrow because of the way her long lashes hang like parasols. Her face is wide, her lips are full and glistening and just barely parted. Betty is more severe, angling forward. Her hair twists into a tight bun. Her nose is raised to a height that affects snobbery. Her lashes curve up like the sharp edges of a porcupine's fear-stricken back. And then there is Jane who looks moribund. Poppy, of late, spends all of his time with this one. Her hair is bobbed and hangs in her face, which is fallen and disturbed and nearly violent. The corners of her mouth slightly arch; the rim of her nose slightly flares. Otherwise, her eyes are hollow; they are dark and hollow, fully indulged in the heavy mood of the shade.

The glass cabinets encasing Poppy's aircraft line the outer corridors of the entire thirty-third floor. They hold thousands of planes, each of whose creases was crafted by Poppy with much care. When the old man snaps one away with his brittle wrist, his expression constricts and he looks as though he calculates the angles of ascent, counts the seconds the wings remain aloft, contemplates the pull of gravity on the nose. I occasionally see him watch me lift a plane from the border of linoleum on the periphery of his chambers. As I pinch the fuselage and delicately place it on a silver tray, I can feel his eyes wince when the belly's fold touches my reflection in the metal.

A tall shaft of white fluorescent light emanates from the kitchen's doorway. The countertops, tabletops, and floor glow white. Everything glows and sparkles and turns at ninety degree angles. The sink, the refrigerator, the stove, all the appliances are polished, stainless and brushed steel—the cabinets, the preparation areas, the doors to the dozen pantries as well. The windows are spotless. The intensity of the kitchen's light forces the night into an opaque reflection of the room's glow.

I enter the "Medical Supplies" pantry containing Poppy's medical supplies. It is a small room unto itself—six feet wide and twelve feet long. White lacquered storage units with shelves and cupboards run the length of the walls on both sides. The bottom of the door is magnetized, as is the wall, so that when I walk in, the door remains ajar.

Next door to "Medical Supplies" is "Sterilization," a much larger room, a room almost the size of the kitchen, which is quite large, at least several hundred square feet. Mr. Lutherford and Mr. Heinrik, the sterilization attendants, share a shift, during which time they sanitize all of Poppy's utensils, pots, pans, pens, paper, sheets, smocks, masks, and an entire host of miscellany that is necessary to decontaminate before it enters Poppy's presence.

I open a cupboard on the wall that "Medical" shares with "Sterilization" in order to retrieve a Ziploc storage bag.

"Do you know him?"

It is Mr. Lutherford. Even muffled through the thin wall, Mr. Lutherford's voice is very distinct. As is Mr. Heinrik's. Mr. Lutherford's resonates from his barrel chest and is very deep and coarse. Mr. Heinrik's voice is soft and terse. The two men babble incessantly, constantly pushing the boundaries of authorized speech.

"Do you know him?" Mr. Lutherford repeats.

"No, I'm afraid not," Mr. Heinrik responds.

"You say he diverted funds?"

"More than you can imagine."

"I have heard laundering."

"There are a number of accountants under him, all under suspicion."

"Is there a name?"

"Blank."

"Blank?"

"Yes, that's his name. Blank. Mortimer Blank."

"Never heard of him."

"He must be Internal Affairs."

"No further access then."

"I'm surprised they've disclosed as much as they have."

"It's too bad."

"Yes, too bad."

The two men pause for a moment.

"What is the news?" I ask through the cupboard as I dip Poppy's tray into a square pan full of rubbing alcohol.

"Mr. Louse?" they say in unison.

"Yes."

"Since when are you interested in the news?" Mr. Heinrik asks.

"Mr. Louse interested in the news?" Mr. Lutherford echoes.

"I'm only interested in wishing you two a good evening," I say, not really wanting to have anything to do with their conversation. Although I must keep up with the latest news, I like to stay uninvolved. It's my way. I merely like to let them know I'm here, listening.

"You'll be delighted to hear that there is nothing to report, Mr. Louse," Mr. Heinrik says.

"Tonight we are surrounded by angels such as yourself," says Mr. Lutherford.

"He'll have his wings any day now, no doubt. The first into Paradise."

"No doubt."

"Just wanted to let you know I was here," I say as I remove a Ziploc storage bag from a shelf.

"As usual," they say in unison.

"Until later," I say.

"Yes, later," they say.

I click the cupboard closed.

Their voices disappear.

I retrieve the used syringe, place it into the Ziploc bag, and dispose of it in the incinerator at the very back of the room. The rubber tubing, which I wrap around Poppy's limbs, is to be left coiled and dropped into a separate tub of rubbing alcohol. The bottle full of his elixir is to be placed in a cupboard on the opposite wall, marked "Pharmaceuticals." I am then instructed to shut the door and go to my quarters.

My quarters are exactly twice the dimensions of the pantry. They are located near the northern corner of the eastern wing alongside the other quarters demarcated for domestic personnel. The walls are bare, painted white; the floors are covered in white tiles. I have a twin bed made up of a box spring and mattress. A skylight looks up to evening constellations. During the day it is covered with a scrim that filters out the brightness and the heat. It mechanically closes at daybreak and opens after dusk. Under the skylight is a desk, which is situated near the entrance to the bathroom, where I have my own toilet, private shower, cleaning supplies, wash basin, and incinerator. Red camera surveillance lights blink in all corners of the room and the bathroom.

There is a small hole in the wall near my bed through which I can watch my neighbor Mr. Crane, the maintenance engineer, and through which he can watch me. I rarely look in on him, however. I have no idea how often he looks in on me. Theoretically, we can look in on each other at any time, though never simultaneously. When this occurs, the hole turns black, and we therefore know the other is present. We must then follow the contract, which states: *staff members must forfeit their voyeurism for the remainder of the day and/or night.* This has happened to me and Mr. Crane just once.

Usually he isn't in. Only on several occasions have I caught him at home, pacing the floors of his cramped quarters, reclining on his bed, getting ready for his duties. I will look through the hole when I am in search of entertainment. Thus far, however, Mr. Crane has provided me very little. Other than the fact that his head has an unusual oblong shape that casts conic shadows onto the wall, I find him very dull. He tends to sit on the edge of his bed and look out his skylight, even when there is nothing to be seen.

When I reach my quarters, I sit at my desk, do a check of the procedure as I glance down at the section of my contract regarding Poppy's tray. I am to keep this section of the contract laminated and in the upper left-hand drawer of the desk along with a syringe full of a drug with which, twice daily, I am to inject myself in the thigh. It slows my heart rate and makes me a little faint. I do not know what purpose it serves. All I know is that I am to inject myself with it once in the late morning and once at night. If and only if I am convinced that I have successfully inoculated myself, can I remove my gloves from my hands, the mask from my face, the smock from my body, and drop these things down the incinerator installed in my bathroom.

I take a few moments at the wash basin to allow the dizziness to pass as I look at my reflection in the mirror, wondering how Mr. Crane perceives me as he looks through his hole. I too am not a very handsome man and must seem as dull to him as he seems to me. I can surmise from the lines around my eyes and above my brow, from the few gray hairs sprouting off my chest, that I am, perhaps, in my midthirties. I have thin cheeks and a short chin. My nose is somewhat aquiline, but not exactly beak-like. My eyes are brown and almond shaped and my ears are unusually large. My body is fit, but not well-defined. My hands are somehow too large for my body and my thumbs are slightly deformed; they are bent at the joint, turning inward against my index fingers. Small bones protrude from the joints like warts, and are callused over from the motion of rubbing them against my palms.

Contrary to what my physiognomy would suggest, I am very adroit and have very keen hand-eye coordination. If I am able to present Mr. Crane or my anonymous observers any kind of thrill, it is when I hunt flies, the ones that find their way into our quarters through the air conditioning vents. We are required to hunt them; something I take great pleasure in, unlike Mr. Crane, who allows the flies to buzz around his quarters until they are nearly dead from boredom. He sits on his bed with his swatter in hand and makes exhausted and fake attempts to hunt his prey. I, on the other hand, find the hunt stimulating and take it seriously. One might assume that the buzzing and the banging against the walls and the skylight in search of freedom would make me feel uncomfortable. But not at all. Just the opposite. I look forward to their arrival. In fact, I await their arrival with great anticipation. I have in my desk drawer, beside my contract, a regulation fly swatter to be used on such occasions. I run and jump and crawl and feel a great rush when I finally corner a pest. Against what I initially believed when I first took up this avocation, there are many ways a fly swatter will weigh down upon its prey. I have caught flies by their hind legs, by a wing. I have turned many into one winged flies and managed, on a few occasions, to catch them by their remaining wing. I have felt great pride watching flies with no wings run and jump off their hind legs, only to land on their faces. I have splattered flies and decapitated them. To splatter a fly in one straight shot, I have discovered, isn't nearly as entertaining as breaking it down bit by bit, wing by leg by head. Since the first day I was escorted to my quarters, I have sent three hundred twenty-three flies down the incineration chute to the fire. I have killed flies on every wall, under my bed, in the shower, and the sink. I have even splattered one directly on the lens of a surveillance camera. I have had perverse thoughts of eating flies and more respectable thoughts of collecting them. I would like to label and pin them to rows of Styrofoam and catalogue them in wooden drawers. Of course, I would never be allowed. But I do relish the idea. I can't help but wonder whether if I had any concrete memories of the past, I would be fascinated with such things. But the fact of the matter is that I don't. I don't know why this is, or why it has to be. I have asked. I have asked and I have been ignored and have been dealt with. So I stopped asking after some time. Now, among other things, I chase flies when I am away from my duties.

When the dizziness from my injection passes, I wash my hands and my face with surgical scrub, then change my shoes and my uniform. I send the smock, mask, and rubber gloves down the incinerator chute and continue toward the interoffice elevator bank in order to gather supplies for the midnight movie.

What I have just completed should take me no more than nine minutes and thirty seconds. *Should an attendant think of taking half steps or shortcuts through this procedure, he can be demoted up to .5 percent against his debt. The current yield on his debt will appreciate X months later than current appreciation date. Number of months are determined by the level of the infraction.*

The regulation of half steps and shortcuts applies to all procedures for which all staff members are responsible. It is known as the

"Liability Doctrine." In short, if any half step or shortcut is taken through any procedure, we are liable for our lack of thoroughness and/or attention to detail, even when such thoroughness and/or attention to detail is dependent on another staff member. This dependency on other staff members makes for *interdependence*.

Every week since I have been Poppy's ward, I have been suffering from a lack of interdependence. I have been demoted once a week for as long as I can remember because Poppy's exterminator has never appeared in Poppy's chambers to perform his duties. And since the exterminator and I are considered a full step — I, half the step, he, the other half — my efforts cannot be completed in full. According to my contract, I am to escort the exterminator through the corridors, into the bathrooms, and through Poppy's living quarters. Every third Thursday of the month, at exactly 9:00 P.M., I am to wait in one of the three corridors leading to Poppy's chambers. I am to wait until either Poppy calls for me, or until I am supposed to be somewhere else. Not once has the exterminator shown up, and not once have I heard of an investigation into the exterminator.

I do not understand why there hasn't been any investigation; especially since Poppy has seen, on more than several occasions, a small beetle crawling in and out of the various ravines of his chambers' landscape. When I tell Poppy that the exterminator has been neglecting his duties, he tells me about the Communist diaspora and the nature of the Mongol hordes of the thirteenth century. He often talks at length about the ruthless attacks Genghis Khan led on a fortress in Bukhara in the region of Central Asia. He will condemn the Mongols in both the Chinese and Russian governments, blame them for these regimes' obstinacy throughout the centuries.

When he is through with his discourse, I ask him what should be done. He says he doesn't want me to do anything. In fact, he warns me that I am not to speak about such things until he, himself, sees the insect with his own eyes. And when this occurs, I am not supposed to contact the exterminator, but rather am expected to chase after the bug, capture it, and send it down the incinerator. But every time he has seen this beetle, I haven't. I tell him so. Regardless, I am sent off to attack this invisible creature, dig for it with my fingers, through the refuse of headlines and history, tear away words upon his commands. I destroy the mountain range as I know it, rearrange it so that it looks like a wrecking crew has stripped the land of all its precious qualities. He points me in this direction and that direction until he tires from the chase and I'm left panting and sweating and have newsprint and paper cuts covering my hands.

I discovered early on that Poppy is deathly afraid to be in the same room with another's blood, which I find confusing, because he is so exacting when describing the details of medieval weaponry and how, with the proper amount of brute force, a thick and heavy sword cuts through skin and crushes bone, whereupon a man is a pulsing corpse. On the several occasions I have bled in his presence, he has informed Celia Lonesome, Head of Domestic Staff, to send a cleaning crew to disinfect his chambers. During this time he remains in bed as the workmen clean around him, spraying heavy doses of ammonia onto the newspapers and into the air. Dressed in smocks, masks, and rubber gloves, the crew disinfects and scours until they have depleted most of the chambers' oxygen. The old man takes deep breaths, which calms him of his terror. And, mind you, his terror is quite real. I have learned that he has many fears like this, and if one wished to torment him it would be a very simple chore. If there was a man of action and malicious deeds who didn't care about his fate, he could threaten Poppy's sanity with a simple pitcher of rain water. I have learned that it isn't so much the blood, although it is the blood, but more that blood is liquid. He fears most forms of liquids—to see them, drink them, touch them, be in their presence. He is convinced that liquids in general, especially water, and even water purified by the staff, is contaminated. He has a similar aversion to fresh fruits, meats, and vegetables. He says, "the grit of the earth, the dew of the morning, the fertilizers, are full of infectious bacteria, bacteria imperceptible to the eye, deadly and unspeakably unfriendly."

Poppy's personal clerical staff sit in fish bowl cubicles under white fluorescent rods. A labyrinth of small offices and passages recesses into the northern-most quadrant of the building. Fingers type furiously. Telephone receivers simultaneously lift and fall.

I enter a door that leads to an interoffice elevator and swipe my identification card through an electronic eye, then punch in my code. The elevator's reflective silver doors open into a reflective silver interior. I press B1. The doors close. The elevator drops, and I can feel the rapid descent in the core of my stomach. I ride down thirty-three floors and exit through Accounting, which, like the offices in the penthouse, recesses deep into the back of the building, only deeper. Large stacks of bundled greenbacks meticulously line the desks of the swing shift money managers, the ones who work through all hours of the night to take advantage of the international markets. I pass through a glass-encased corridor and watch the faces of the men and women as their lips incessantly mutter indistinguishable syllables. They thrust them into the air in a very strategic and deadly serious manner characterized by pursed lips and indented brows.

A small group of men and women dressed in our standard uniform of gray suits, gray vests, blue ties, black belts, black shoes, huddle together in the passageway. They are huddled so tightly I can't make out a single face. Their voices remain compressed within their circle.

"Have you been implicated?"

"I couldn't say. What about you?"

"I'm not sure. But I wouldn't rule it out."

"We can never rule it out."

"Guilty by design."

"Yes, guilty by design."

"It's just hard to say what may come of it."

"Especially when they're still making assessments."

"The future is in the hands of the present."

"So they say."

"It will come out soon enough."

"Of course."

"Of course."

"He will…"

"They say…"

"…forget…"

"…go."

"…us…"

And the voices drift as I reach the end of the hall.

The hallway ends.

I open a door that leads to a narrow glass-paned hall identical to the one I just left. Lights illuminate the money counters sorting through crane-loads of coins laid out in mounds on glass tables. I take a corridor to the right, then the left, through a double security door guarded by an individual behind dark tinted glass, and then down another flight of stairs, which deposits me into a large subterranean warehouse where the noise of forklifts and other heavy machinery begins to make itself known to my ears. Beside the door is a row of chairs. A line of teenagers looking approximately the same age sit in demure silence. The one closest to the door stands to attention.

"Yes, sir!" he says to me with a stiff upper lip. He recognizes that I am a domestic from my shaved head and arms. His hand starts to shake a little—he knows who I work for.

"Please retrieve the following," I say to the boy as I hand him a prewritten list of items I need.

"Yes, sir!" he says. His youthful legs sprint down the long corridor into the supply room.

As I wait for him to return, one boy begins whispering into another boy's ear, and the next thing I know they are all whispering to each other.

"They revealed some names."

"The ones under Blank?"

"Yes. Berger, Lumpit, Nester, and Blurd."

"Blurd?"

"Yes, Blurd."

"Anyone else?"

"No."

"But there are more to come."

"Anything concrete?"

"Their books were confiscated."

"Yes, that I heard."

"They're being reviewed."

"They say many others."

"Many names."

"Yes, they'll follow."

"Found in a vault, they say."

"In a trunk."

"In a vault."

"They will no doubt find others."

"There is no telling how far up it will go."

"I have heard a woman in Internal Affairs."

"Let go to Sales."

"They have the most evidence on her."

"Nothing shredded."

"Nothing hidden."

"It was all there in plain light."

"They say she confessed."

"I wonder how long it will be before the viewing?"

"It shouldn't be long."

"It could be any time now."

"Is there any other news?"

"Only that it's big."

"Bigger than ever before."

"Our lives are to be affected."

"Changed."

"Never to be the same again."

"Our path to Paradise might be…"

"To be kept from Paradise…"

"It just might be."

"A great disappointment."

"So it seems."

"Yes."

"Yes yes."

When the boy returns with my order everyone becomes silent. I look at them.

They look at me.

"Very well done," I say to the boy.

He hands back my list, on which is stamped "Received." He hands over six black and six blue pens (all of which are individually shrink-wrapped and inspected for noticeable perforations), four yellow legal pads (also individually shrink-wrapped), and a *Wall Street Journal* wrapped in a plastic bag with a red twisty tie at the top (each page has been lightly misted with disinfectant). I ask the boy's name because I am impressed with his diligence.

"Venison, sir!"

"Good work, Venison."

I briskly walk away from the boys to show them my diligence is not unlike theirs, that I too have an authority to whom I must bow. I can hear their whispers turn into plain speech as I depart. It follows me through the narrow passageway until I am several hundred feet beyond them.

When I reach Bathroom Number Three, I first place the newly gathered objects on a tray whose specific purpose is for the bathroom's preparation. I remove a pair of sterilized rubber gloves from a supply closet resembling the medical supply pantry in the kitchen and put them on. I remove the *Wall Street Journal* from its package and unfold it. I go to the center page and lay the fold over the newspaper rack built into the wall for such a purpose. I leave each pen and pad in its shrink-wrap and place these items on a shelf below the rack. From Bathroom Number Three's supply closet, I remove a sterilized phone from its shelf along with a cord, which like everything else is wrapped in plastic. I place these things on top of a recently overhauled Zenith and roll everything in front of the toilet. I remove the cord from the bag, plug it into the phone and click the attachment into the wall. I place the phone with the cord neatly coiled next to the toilet on a little foot-stool. I run into the bathroom supply closet and open a new box of Kleenex, which I place next to the phone. I reach into my pocket and remove my tape measure. I measure three feet from the head of the toilet outward to the center of the room. I roll the television over the marble floor to the spot I have visually marked, and plug the power cord into an outlet near Jane's facade above the sink. I run to the toilet with the remote control in hand and place it on the left-hand armrest. I crouch down and lift the receiver of the phone. I dial Godwin Beeles at the television station.

"Beeles here."

"12 A.M.," I say and hang up. He knows the procedure.

I collect all of the debris and send it down the incineration chute in the supply closet and walk to the kitchen where I am to observe the Head of Domestic Staff, Celia Lonesome, prepare Poppy's meal.

When I reach the kitchen, a plastic package of rice bobs up and down in a pot of boiling water. Poppy's silver dinner tray rests beside the stove. It contains a brilliantly shining can, a medium-sized pot, a Pyrex bowl, a package of silverware, freshly bleached cotton napkins, and a can opener. Ms. Lonesome exits Food Pantry Number Four carrying a can of peaches. She greets me with the smile with which we are to greet one another.

"Good evening, Mr. Louse."

"Good evening, Ms. Lonesome."

I look into her light blue eyes, which are translucent and void of any visible curiosity. The bright fluorescent light of the kitchen reflects off her smooth white skin. Her face is round and shows no revealing signs of age or expression. Unlike Mr. Heinrik and Mr. Lutherford, Ms. Lonesome has no distinct intonations or patterns of speech. She stresses her vowels as if they're not there. Her consonants click against her palate and her lips without enthusiasm, as if she isn't talking at all. Each utterance triggers no recollection of any time or place in my forgotten past. In fact, her mouth hardly moves when she talks. I sometimes feel as if she is throwing her voice straight to my brain, and we are talking telepathically.

"Have you heard the news, Mr. Louse?"

"No, Ms. Lonesome. Not in full."

Ms. Lonesome gently and slowly rocks the can of peaches between her palms, against the front of her blouse.

"Intelligence has discovered the source of the missing funds," she says softly. "The money has been attached to Mr. Blank. Mortimer Blank. Who they believe laundered the money with the assistance of a small group of accountants and Intelligence officers. Pan Opticon reports that Paradise may be threatened. It is very worrisome, Mr. Louse."

"Yes, I agree, Ms. Lonesome. Very worrisome."

Ms. Lonesome looks at me blankly.

I look at Ms. Lonesome with what feels like longing.

Ms. Lonesome turns away.

I could, at this juncture, inquire if she knows anything of Mr. Blank. But I generally find that the obvious questions are always the questions that never have answers. So I refrain from asking.

Ms. Lonesome leans over the kitchen wash basin. She lifts a scrub brush and applies it to the can of peaches. She turns on the water and scrubs. Her motions, like her language, are confident and reassuring. She scrubs the metallic container until all remnants of the adhesive once holding the wrapper are gone. She scrubs until the canister is shining. She wipes. She polishes with a fresh paper towel and places the can on the tray next to the other can. She goes to the stove and with one hand removes the package of rice with a pair of tongs, and with the other wipes the water from the plastic with a paper towel. She carefully molds the hot package of rice onto the bottom of the Pyrex bowl, and then walks about the kitchen collecting all the paper goods, which she disposes of in the incinerator next to the sink.

The tray is prepared, all but for the beverage.

Ms. Lonesome walks to Refrigerator Number Three and removes a sanitized bottle of grape flavored NeHi. It is the only beverage Poppy will drink. Ms. Lonesome places the bottle onto the tray, takes hold of the silver handles and walks toward me and then past me into the obscurity of the western wing. She delicately steps on the linoleum floor so as not to make noise with her heels. Her posture is very good and her uniform is crisp. She really is the most outstanding staff member by all means, a good example to us all.

Poppy's euphoria has worn off by the time Ms. Lonesome and I enter his chambers. He is in the very center of the bed curled into a tight ball. Upon seeing us, he struggles to his knees, sounding a barely audible groan. I retreat to the shadows of the northwest corner of the room as Ms. Lonesome places the tray of food on the eastern night table and proceeds to slip on a pair of rubber gloves. Meanwhile, the package of rice collects condensation and steams through the dull red streaks of the surveillance cameras.

"Now, Ms. Lonesome," Poppy says in a broken voice.

"Yes, Mr. Blackwell."

Ms. Lonesome removes the pot from the tray and places it before Poppy. She hands him the box of Kleenex, from which he grabs two large fistfuls of tissue. Ms. Lonesome takes hold of Poppy's frail arm and shoulder as he secures himself over the silver rim. I can see Ms. Lonesome hold her breath as Poppy takes one, and I can see her continue to hold it as Poppy, in one retch, vomits a tablespoon of black bile into the pot. Ms. Lonesome continues to hold her breath as Poppy waits for the pain to subside. He positions himself in anticipation for more. But tonight no more comes.

His muscles go slack.

Ms. Lonesome pulls the pot away.

Poppy falls into his pillow.

Ms. Lonesome, with pot in hand, silently exits the chambers.

NTROLLING PA

Herbert Horatio Blackwell was born into humble, but dignified, beginnings. His family resided in the oil town of H., located near the Buffalo Bayou, the marshy tributary linking S. and T. His father was a sheriff and fortune seeker, his mother, a refined debutante from D. who longed to return to her family home. Although Mr. Blackwell's mother found H. uncivilized, barren, and desperate, she dutifully stuck with her husband and child. She remained silent as the town fell into a postboom decline, when H.'s brackish waters became contaminated with decomposing cattle rejected by the stockyards. Small pox and typhoid fever spread and became recurrent epidemics killing many young children. She watched as yellow fever quarantines appeared on doors across the district and black rot, canker, and elm disease denuded the landscape. Incinerator fires burned all day and night as the noise of drills wound around in their derricks.

Mr. Blackwell's mother became so affected by these conditions, she was terrified of all small and large animals alike and obsessed with the perils of mosquitoes, roaches, flies, and beetles. She locked herself away from the stench of sulfur rising from the tidal marshes, the odor of mud, silt, and oil. Only on crisp winter days would she take the young Mr. Blackwell out walking, during which time she made him write down all the miserable sights she saw, including the sickly children wandering through town with fever in their eyes. Her lists of abysmal visions grew long and tedious and she began dreaming of mice carrying plagues that crept into her food. She dreamed the oil from the fields rained down on her house. She dreamed of typhoid and tuberculosis, yellow and scarlet fevers, dripping through the roof tiles.

Meanwhile Mr. Blackwell's father enforced order on H. He chained his prisoners to trees and let them wait in the rain for the prison wagons to arrive. During his idle time, he staged cockfights with outlaw wildcatters and spent days whoring around with his brother, gambling away small fortunes, falling over drunk in saloons. In his spare time, he conceived inventions. He patented designs for oil derricks, machine shops, and tools. His greatest conceit was a drill bit that revolutionized the oil industry and made his family wealthy for as long as there is a future. The drill bit was nothing anyone had seen before—a small ribbed device with one hundred sixty-six edges that turned both clockwise and counterclockwise. It easily burrowed through the layers of earth separating the rigs from the oil.

The young Mr. Blackwell's mother, unfortunately, never enjoyed this wealth. Her nerves grew worse. She longed more and more to return to D. to be with her mother. And then one day, when she went for an examination, her doctor discovered a growth in her womb, which she was convinced was caused by the cattle and the vermin. Before the doctor determined whether or not the growth was cancerous, she insisted that he remove it. Every night she was having nightmares of larvae infesting her body. Once the doctor heard of this, and after Mr. Blackwell's father and uncle exerted their influence, the doctor agreed to perform the surgery.

Mr. Blackwell said good-bye to his mother. She was dressed like a lady. She remained indifferent to his crying and patted him on the head and kissed his cheek farewell.

His mother's womb hemorrhaged in the middle of the procedure. With her weak heart, she died on the table.

Several years later, the nightmares of Mr. Blackwell's mother found their way to his father. His father was more silent about what he saw, nevertheless he died as abruptly as Mr. Blackwell's mother. Mr. Blackwell was eighteen at the time. He inherited the family tool business and took it on only long enough to make arrangements to leave H. and go west, away from the torment of his parents' ill fate. He left the business in the hands of his uncle, sold the family house, and boarded a train bound for L. where he began flying and designing planes, a lifelong dream he acquired while patiently attending to his mother. From her bedroom window he enjoyed watching the biplanes lift into the sky from the distant airfield and fly over the town of H.

Shortly after arriving in L., he began racing his planes in land speed competitions across the desert. He flew entire lengths of states, then two, then three. He broke land-speed records everywhere he went. Eventually, he designed a plane for great distances and traveled the entire width of the North American continent nonstop. People fell out onto the streets to celebrate his arrival. They had ticker-tape parades for him in all the great cities. By the time he traveled back across the country he had become a household name. He was visited by dignitaries from around the world and entertained by all the celebrities and movie moguls of the day.

After so much hardship and suffering, such success was a Gift from God!

As he had become interested in planes, he soon was interested in the technology and spiritual effect of cinema. He began financing films for EKG Productions and eventually bought the studio outright. In the early years, he directed and starred in *H.A. 13-3*, *Trails of the Golden Horde*, and *Custer's Last Stand*; he later produced scores of others. Simultaneously, he continued designing planes and airports and constructed the ubiquitous Transit Air from the bottom up. He carried passengers and cargo to the outer reaches of the world. In times of war his planes carried bombs and armaments to our steadfast soldiers.

Mr. Blackwell was a great triumph! A Patriot! A Hero!

EKG Productions grossed more money than any studio in the history of studios! Transit Air was the most successful commercial airliner in the history of airliners! And so, of course, it came to pass that Mr. Blackwell, a man not meant to rest easily, moved on to his next incredible feat: the Resort Town of G.! Our home and refuge! The most triumphant triumph Mr. Blackwell has ever triumphed!

God Bless Herbert Horatio Blackwell!

God Bless Him!

3. THE FIRST NIGHT

THE FIRST NI

The first night I arrived in the Resort Town of G., I was held in a small cell whose walls were draped with burgundy velvet curtains. There was no furniture other than the metal folding chair in which I was sitting, a metal folding chair across from me, and a claw foot oak table between me and the chair. Sitting in the center of the table was a VCR whose wires ran to a corner of the room, around the back of a large television. A bare bulb hung from the ceiling and garishly illuminated the sheen of the velvet wall-cover. My vision, at this point, was impaired. Everything appeared as if it were submerged in water.

A man dressed in a gray flannel suit and a white dress shirt pushed back the curtain and walked in. He was carrying a briefcase, which he set down beside the VCR. From an inside jacket pocket he removed a plastic bottle, opened it up, and walked over to me. He placed one hand on the nape of my neck and with the other hand delivered the pungent bitter smell of the bottle's contents to my nose. A great force rushed to my head, snapping it back into his palm. In a moment, my vision cleared and I could see the man's severe countenance. He was middle-aged; his skin was tight, rippled with thin pink lines. He looked weather-beaten, but not from the sun. Rather it was the lack of sun that gave him his appearance— capillaries surfaced on his dry and pallid complexion, deep crow's-feet fanned the corners of his eyes. What's more, a thin scar, inflicted by a fine knife or a wire, circled his throat. It ran just above his shirt line and over his Adam's apple, which looked like a fish skimming the surface of the water. His Adam's apple swam up and down as if tethered by the scar, which gauged the rise and fall of his voice's tonality.

"Do you know why you're here, Mr. Louse?" he asked.

"No," I said. My voice sounded hoarse. I realized it was because I was parched. "May I have something to drink?" I asked nervously.

All of a sudden another man, much larger than the man sitting before me, walked from behind the curtain. He was gripping a glass of water in a hairy fist. He too was wearing a gray flannel suit with a white dress shirt and looked as weary as his colleague. He placed the water on the table and walked back behind the curtain. With my hand trembling uncontrollably, I reached for the glass and gulped it down. I coughed some up and spilled some on my clothes, which, I realized at that moment, were exactly the same as these two men's.

"Do you know where you are, Mr. Louse?"

"No," I said. "Where am I?"

He ignored me.

The man opened his briefcase. He dabbed his finger tips with his tongue and started shuffling through papers. He then removed a notebook and began to take notes.

"Who are you?" I asked.

"Bender. Internal Affairs. That was Mr. Godmeyer, my associate. You've dug yourself into quite a deep hole, Mr. Louse."

"Am I dead?" I asked, feeling frightened that I was, in fact, dead. My body felt numb and Mr. Bender, who was directly across from me, sounded as though his voice were traveling from a great distance away. In addition to this, it occurred to me that I had no recollection of being brought to this place. As hard as I searched, nothing surfaced.

Mr. Bender looked at me curiously as if pondering my question. "In a manner of speaking."

"In what manner of speaking?"

"You owe us a lot of money," he said flatly.

"I do?"

"Maybe you think you'd be better off?" he said, his pen poised as if he were ready to write my response.

"If I were dead?"

"Let me be the first to tell you, it's just not the case, Mr. Louse. Not at all. I've got terms here. Terms I think you and any other reasonable man would appreciate," he said, tapping his briefcase.

"How much is it exactly? The amount that I owe you."

"The figure isn't important, Mr. Louse."

"I just can't remember. How is it I owe you this money?"

"Mr. Louse. We both know the trouble you're in. I don't need to make it more obvious than it needs to be."

"Please, if you don't mind telling me."

And then he started talking faster than I could follow. I didn't know what to say. I didn't understand why he was doing what he was doing. It merely made me look into his eyes, which were dark and full of my reflection, which I didn't recognize. He continued speaking but I didn't listen to him. The sounds caromed to places in the room other than my ears. I leaned over the table and tried to look deeper to see myself. I felt very weak and passive. I remembered nothing at all, other than my name.

"Mr. Louse," he said, snapping his fingers at me. "Mr. Louse. You entered our casino three weeks ago and showed proof of your holdings in a B. bank account. We confirmed this information with the bank. Based on this, as well as a credit report…"

"Did I authorize a credit report?" I asked.

Mr. Bender reached into his briefcase and took out an authorization form.

"Is this your signature?"

I recognized that it was a signature of my name, but I didn't recognize it. I answered with what must have been a puzzled look. He placed the paper back in his briefcase.

"Based on your account information and your credit report, we decided that you were a worthwhile risk and at your request we authorized an open line of credit at 17.8 percent annual interest. Do you remember signing for this?"

"No," I said as he handed me the form showing me another signature.

"When we tried to close your line of credit, you became very defiant."

"I'm sorry. I don't recall."

"We were forced to call Security and detain you in a holding cell on the premises. You calmed down and allowed Dr. Felonius Barnum, our in-house specialist, to examine you for a nervous condition."

"A doctor?"

"Dr. Barnum, our in-house specialist. He treated you at your request for the past several weeks while you recuperated in one of our rooms. To spare you any more public humiliation, you requested that we treat you for your gambling disorder with whatever therapies we thought most effective."

"I did?"

"You signed a release form."

"I did?"

"You did." Bender pulled the release form out of his briefcase and put it on the table. "You also signed a letter of intent, agreeing to consider services you could provide in exchange for your debt. After consulting with one of our in-house counselors, as well as a member of the credit union, you agreed that our terms were fair, and in the long run would be most beneficial to your future. You then signed this initial contract," he said, pulling it out of the briefcase, "the nature of which I don't need to remind you will eventually relieve you of your debt, provide you with stock options in the organization, and give you a brand new line of credit as well as other undisclosed benefits that will become known to you as you ascend to the plateau of accumulating disposable income."

Bender sorted through a long list of items on the paper trail; he provided examples of all he talked about, and assured me that other forms of evidence, including video and audio tape, live witnesses and depositions, were available for me to view at a later time. I didn't insist on anything. I was too dazed, all the time trying to remember what had happened. There was nothing at all that connected me to a larger story. Whatever language I had to describe my thoughts came from someplace a priori. I didn't know why I knew what a release form was, for instance. Or why I cared about a credit report, and how it was that any combination of syllables could run out of my mouth for that matter. The fact that I understood what syllables were seemed somewhat curious to me.

"I want you to know," Bender said, "that we have decided not to press any criminal charges."

"I see," I said, not entirely sure if I wanted to find out what my criminal activity was. "And my criminal activity would be…"

"It is my understanding that when your line of credit went dead you became quite belligerent with one of the pit bosses. When a security guard tried to pull you away, you assaulted her and took her pistol from its holster. You first turned the gun on yourself and then on the pit boss and demanded a bag full of $1,000.00 chips. When the pit boss wouldn't give you what you wanted, you began to threaten his life. It was at this point that plainclothes security agents apprehended you."

"I see," I said, dismayed.

"Would you like to watch the videotape?" he asked.

"If you don't mind."

"As you wish."

He leaned over and pressed the "Play" button on the VCR. A surveillance tape with the time, date, and location showed me, and it was unmistakably me, doing exactly what Bender said I had done. I was relieved when I was able to recognize myself. I was wearing an oxford shirt and trousers and looked no different than any of the others around me. The tape was of very good quality and showed no signs of tampering whatsoever. I tried to recognize the layout of the casino floor, but was unable at this point to separate the greens and the reds of the carpeting.

"Now, Mr. Louse," he said, pressing the "Stop" button, "if you accept our terms, this is what I have to offer."

From his briefcase, he pulled out a diagram with a flow chart of the organization's various components and pointed at it as he gave me a speech about the role I would play as a future trustee.

4. THE FUTURE TRUSTEE

E FUTURE TRU

As a **future trustee**, a ward of the resort town of G. is expected to follow all orders given by higher ranking members as well as precepts written into a social contract. The social contract is a legal document, which is to be signed by the ward as well as counsel witnessing the ward's induction. The social contract is function- and site-specific: Depending on the job the ward is assigned and the floor on which he works and lives, he is to follow a set of respective rules for his individual tasks, as well as a particular set of decorum appropriate for the security level on which he functions. The system is designed so that **future trustees** with the most debt begin their work on the higher floors alongside those with the most stature, so that those with the most stature can observe **newcomers** and decide when these newcomers are to be promoted to the lower floors — a process which moves them closer to eradicating their debt. In theory, debt is not eradicated by **time served**, but rather by **merit gained**, which is based on efficiency and obedience. In other words, in order for a ward to move up he has to move down, and in the process of moving down, he will move up. If the ward follows these guidelines he will not only be eligible to grow beyond the point where his line of credit is restored, but will be granted **trustee** status. With trustee status the ward will be automatically entered into a lottery system in which he will be able to start his ascent to the level of **Officer**, **Manager**, **Middle Manager**, **Executive**, **Member of the Board of Directors**, and **Controlling Partner**, potentially rising one level with each drawing. Simultaneously, he will be entered into a lottery system that goes into effect when the **Executive Controlling Partner** passes away, at which time, lots are drawn and a new leader is randomly chosen from the pool of all organization members.

5. THE BOX OF BUTTERFLIES

BOX OF BUTTE

Footsteps approach in the outer corridor. They approach slowly and softly but are still audible. When they reach the main entrance of Poppy's chambers I find that they belong to the woman I am to call Madame. I assume she is his wife. I do not know her proper name. She appears in Poppy's chambers every night when he is sleeping. She is tall and walks with the graceful posture of a dancer, with her head cocked back, her shoulders square, her arms resting gently at her sides. She is always dressed in mourning from head to toe. I have, therefore, never seen her face. She wears a long and loose black dress, and a veil that only reveals the crescent shape of her eyes. They, and her hands, look like those of a woman much younger than Poppy. When she speaks, her voice is always hushed in a whisper. I am not to ask her anything. I am to provide for her needs and respond only in the way I have been instructed to respond.

When Madame enters the room, she carefully walks over the newspapers, approaches Poppy's bed, and kneels before his sleeping body. She bows her head, clasps her hands together, and begins praying in silence.

After a few moments, she lifts her head.

"Has he asked for me this evening, Mr. Louse?"

"Yes, Madame," I say.

"And what did he say when he spoke of me?"

"He said that 'your radiance and beauty went unmatched by any other and that you were the sole proprietress over his will to live.'"

She looks at Poppy and begins to weep.

"I love him so," she says. "He is my refuge, my heart, my…"

And she weeps some more.

At this point I walk to her side and offer my handkerchief, which I keep in my pants pocket for exactly this task.

She takes the handkerchief from my hand and dabs at her eyes and her nose through the veil.

"You will tell him I love him," she says.

"Of course, Madame. As always."

She raises her head and momentarily looks at me. "Very good, Mr. Louse. Will you please give me a moment alone with him?"

"Of course, Madame."

Madame hands the handkerchief back to me. She bows her head in prayer again and begins humming the third movement of Mozart's "Requiem."

I exit the chambers through the corridor that leads to Bathroom Number Three. I walk between the television and the hologram of Jane and go directly to the incinerator in the supply closet where I dispose of the handkerchief and replace it with a new one.

When I arrive back in Poppy's chambers the woman is gone.

As she does every night, on Poppy's eastern nightstand, she has left behind a narrow glass box filled with three large butterflies.

They are mounted on pins that stick up from a piece of Styrofoam. The wings are extended and rest against the glass. Tonight the butterflies contain the colors of red, yellow, green, and black.

I return to my spot by the wall and listen to the ambient noises of the casino on the television at the foot of Poppy's bed. And as he does every night, Poppy opens his eyes to the butterflies on the table and turns to me.

"Herman?"

"Yes, sir?"

"Did I ask you to wake me?"

"Not to my recollection, sir."

"Then what am I doing awake, Mr. Louse?"

"You woke up, sir."

"On my own?"

"As far as I can tell."

"Is there anything unusual to report at all, Mr. Louse?"

"Nothing unusual, sir."

The old man presses the button of the intercom on his remote control and speaks.

"Mr. Sherwood. Play back last three minutes of my chambers."

The television fades to black. Poppy is asleep in his bed. Madame delicately places the box of butterflies on the table. She gracefully exits the room. I return to my corner. We are motionless. His eyes open. He sits up.

"Herman?"

"Yes, sir?"

"Did I ask you to wake me?"

"Not to my recollection, sir."

"Then what am I doing awake, Mr. Louse?"

"You woke up, sir."

"On my own?"

"As far as I can tell."

"Is there anything unusual to report at all, Mr. Louse?"

"Nothing unusual, sir."

The old man presses the button of the intercom on his remote control.

"One more time, Mr. Sherwood."

The television fades to black. Poppy is asleep in his bed. Madame delicately places the box of butterflies on the table. She gracefully exits the room. I return to my corner. We are motionless. His eyes open. He sits up.

"Herman?"

"Yes, sir?"

"Did I ask you to wake me?"

"Not to my recollection, sir."

"Then what am I doing awake, Mr. Louse?"

"You woke up, sir."

"On my own?"

"As far as I can tell."

"Is there anything unusual to report at all, Mr. Louse?"

"Nothing unusual, sir."

The old man presses the button of the intercom on his remote control.

"Thank you, Mr. Sherwood." He turns to me as he lifts the glass box of butterflies from the night table. "Herman?"

"Yes, sir?"

"Please place the box in the safe."

"Yes, Poppy," I say, fully aware of what's to be done.

He holds out the box of colorful butterflies for me to take away. I step up to his bed and gently remove it from his outstretched hand and cradle it in my arms.

In the middle of the southern wing is a tall and wide wooden coffered door with an iron handle in the shape of a pyramid. I remove the study key from my pocket and insert its silver teeth into the iron latch. When I push the heavy door open it makes a long, scraping sound. It disturbs the stale air of the small vestibule adjoining the larger room, which is separated by an exact duplicate of the door I have just opened, only of smaller dimensions. I close the larger door behind me and step through the smaller door. An electric eye turns on the air conditioning as well as the cameras. Flashing red lights glow in the corners and from the ceiling. I am always tempted to look into one of the cameras to let Mr. Sherwood know that I am aware he is watching me. However, this is considered intolerable behavior. *Becoming self-conscious of the camera defeats the sincerity brought to the act of surveillance. You better serve the staff by remaining candid and forgetting that the cameras are present. To make eye contact with the view finders will be considered an act of defiance. Acting out for the camera is strictly forbidden. You are to maintain an austere respect for the authority of the camera and for those individuals behind it.*

I imagine a pair of passing eyes in a corridor, a stranger's eyes I don't know, nor wish to know. This way if I accidentally do peer into a camera it appears that I am looking through it, as if it is invisible.

Every night when I have the opportunity to walk across this room I catch glimpses of all the objects that inhabit this space, everything that makes the room smell like leather and dust and the timeless decay of the past. I categorize, make an inventory of what I see to remember for later when I am not here: art deco and art nouveau furniture; rolls of carpeting; parts of old movie sets; open cartons filled with Juvenia watches; unsmoked and half-smoked cigarettes; bars of soap; aviation trophies, plaques, and medals; movie equipment; Tiffany lamps; marble statues; ceramic quails; scrap books and articles regarding flying records; footlockers filled with screenplays; pilot logs; a gold cup from a golf tournament; hearing aids; a two volume set of H. G. Wells' *The Outline of History*; a large ceremonial plate from William Randolph Hearst; double breasted suits; white sport coats; leather flight jackets; brown glass medicine bottles; snap-brim Stetson hats; white yachting caps; leather bound law books; piles and piles of white paper memos and yellow legal pads; a solid silver pistol with a note reading: *Captured from Hermann Goering*; German SS binoculars in a black leather case; a cut-glass bowl inscribed: "To Herbert Horatio Blackwell from Hubert Horatio Humphrey"; hundreds of Campbell's soup cans overflowing with canceled personal checks made out to the Brown Derby, The Stork Club, and El Morocco; corporate checks from EKG Productions and Transit Air; a passport; an aged pair of brown wing tip oxfords with curled-up toes.

I enjoy being here for many different reasons; in part, because I can walk slowly and take an inventory of what's here, in part, for the sensation of my feet sinking into thick, plush carpet.

Everywhere else is linoleum and marble.

The carpet makes me feel buoyant and alive. I am able see my footsteps, like fossils, traces of my being. I feel an inexplicable and uncanny sensation of familiarity. I enjoy it so much I begin to hum. It is a melody of my own, one resembling the third movement of

Mozart's "Requiem," but somehow a little different, a little less melancholic, a little bit mirthful even, in a major key.

I walk with light steps, humming, letting the melody build, louder and more complex until it turns into something completely its own, or at least feels to have its own beginning, middle, and end. The intermittent pulse of sound reminds me of a scene from *H.A. 13-3* in which a train, blowing its whistle, slowly winds through a mountain pass. I can clearly see the scene in my mind, and see beyond it, to a distant desert. However, the desert isn't part of the film. In fact, it isn't an image I can ascribe to any place I remember. I try to locate a place for it in my mind, and as I do, the image fades. The desert dissolves. In its place, another image is revealed, this one of myself with a full head of hair. I am reflected in a large tinted window, through which I can see a dry, unobstructed valley expanding and eventually rising into mountains. There is another figure reflected in the window somewhere behind me, but the features of this figure are hazy and distorted and shimmer with motion.

As I walk over the carpeting, I continue to hum this melody, wishing the darkened figure would reveal itself. But the images freeze as I pass a photograph on the wall of a large propeller plane on fire diving down in a spin and a blur over an open meadow. Focused in the foreground, standing shoulder to shoulder, are Poppy and Dr. Barnum. Both of the men are youthful, dressed in flight jackets and khaki pants. Their posture is stiff, their smiles candid. Poppy's hair is short and well groomed. He is clean shaven, all but for a pencil-thin mustache that hugs his upper lip. His eyes are stern, almost shy. He holds a revolver in his right hand. Dr. Barnum holds the tail of a dead opossum over an open ditch.

I immediately stop. I stop humming. I stand motionless. The memory fades as quickly and spontaneously as it came.

Although I don't remember anything within the memoranda that states I should not be humming, humming a tune like the tune I hum as I am ready to inject Poppy with his pharmaceutical, I do not wish… But now…yes, I do remember. I remember a caveat to an old memo, in which he stated that staff members should know better than to mix forms of behavior appropriate to one particular task with similar forms of behavior associated with a completely different task. It would be performing what he considers an act of free will, *a variation of [his] aesthetic*, which is considered as much a form of defiance as sneaking a peek into the camera.

I move. I move quickly. I go directly to the safe without trying to show any signs of haste or guilt, anything out of the ordinary. I dial the combination, open the door, walk in, and deposit the box among the hundreds of other boxes exactly like it—all containing butterflies of varying colors.

There is no need to report my negligence. By now it has undoubtedly been noted. I will be fined accordingly. There is part of me that believes I should report my negligence; however, in no official capacity am I responsible for reporting it. Poppy takes great pride in the accuracy of his surveillance system and all those who work to enforce it. Admission of my guilt, therefore, as ethical as my intention might be, in actuality, may prove to be counterintuitive in producing a more sympathetic conclusion. And so, I can only surmise that silence is the most sensible response. Besides, there is the slightest chance that what I did went unnoticed; or perhaps what I did will be judged with compassion and immediately dismissed. It is impossible to say.

I exit the study, lock the door, and walk the southern wing. I put the humming in a major key out of my head, I replace it with its proper minor key until all resonance of the impure melody is comfortably forgotten.

. HOUSE CALL

When I return to Poppy's chambers, there is a loud explosion in the distance. The room rocks back and forth. Dr. Barnum is standing before the bed with his hands clasped behind his back. Poppy is no longer conscious. Two male attendants stand against the eastern wall holding three rolls of blueprints each. They look like twins, but aren't. They are both the same height and width, with boyish features, dark hair, light eyes, and sallow skin. They stand motionless and stare straight ahead.

Dr. Felonius Barnum is one of the few individuals outside domestic staff that visits Poppy on a regular basis. He is a handsome, elderly man with a trim, rectangular figure. He wears a finely sculpted beard, horn-rimmed glasses, and is always dressed in a nicely pressed pinstripe suit and a pair of glowingly polished, white and black wing tips. Based on the photograph in the study and on the EKG Productions in which Dr. Barnum appeared in his youth, it seems to me that the doctor has aged well. He is still fit and dapper, and though he doesn't have nearly as smooth a complexion as he did when he was a young man, he barely has a wrinkle that isn't flattering to his disposition.

Dr. Barnum usually comes by during the swing shift, between 11:30 P.M. and 6:00 A.M., when Poppy is most alert. They will often discuss various aspects of Paradise and then turn to the TV. They watch old movies I call into Godwin Beeles at the television station at the beginning of the evening. It isn't uncommon for Poppy to pick the 1947 EKG Production of *Dying With No Tomorrow in Sight*, a melodrama about a blind Christian folk singer and his semiretarded wife whose child, a brilliant musical prodigy, is dying of leukemia. The film stars Felonius Barnum as Dr. Felonius Barnum, the brilliant and determined young doctor incapable of curing this young girl's fatal illness. There are many close-ups of Dr. Barnum's moistened, haggard eyes as he looks down onto the bed at his ailing patient. Somber horns and strings rise through apologies and consultations as montages of the young girl's musical genius flash back to more glorious times. Dr. Barnum battles until the very end of the film, when the story reaches its climax and the doctor throws his hands over his face and barges out of the hospital room. The mother, distraught and inconsolable, guides the blind father to a bed post, then falls over the dead little girl. A close-up of the mother's face reveals strange contortions as she holds up her daughter's hands and pretends that the child is once again playing a piano concerto.

More often than not, when Dr. Barnum visits, he and Poppy watch the patrons in the casino downstairs on the closed circuit network. With the Zenith Space Commander in hand, Poppy flips from the roulette wheel to the craps table, to blackjack, baccarat, and the slot machines. They mostly search for desperate faces, for losers who have fear in their eyes, the ones groping for their wallets and begging the cashiers for a new line of credit. Poppy will wait to find a close-up of a face or a manner just like this. And when he does, the two old men linger over it with their eyes. They don't say a word to each other. They simply invite it into their stillness and sit with it in silence.

Tonight, however, Dr. Barnum appears to have come to discuss Paradise. Once a week, as a rule, he retrieves the blueprints of Paradise from Mr. Moorcraft, the Head Engineer, and delivers them to Poppy's chambers. They then discuss the updated designs, the most recent acquisitions, the deals that need to be made, and so on and so forth. Though I have never seen one of the diagrams, I know that Paradise is Poppy's greatest endeavor to date and is the origin of all the intermittent explosions in the distance. We are told that with each detonation we are brought closer to Paradise and the closer we are brought to Paradise the more secure we will be in our futures. The more G. sways with the violent thrust of the detonations the nearer we come to realizing another of Poppy's accomplishments, and thus, the closer to fortune we come. What's more, we have been promised that all of us who achieve trustee status upon Paradise's completion are secured a place in its wings.

"Bring me that chair over there, Mr. Louse," Dr. Barnum orders.

"Yes, sir."

I walk to the southwest corner and retrieve the chair. I carry it over the papers to where the doctor is standing. I nestle the legs into a brochure, a tuft of tissue, and several dailies with the same picture of a rocket ship lifting away from the earth, plumes of fire billowing over the crowns of palm trees.

Dr. Barnum stretches a pair of rubber gloves over his hands, takes hold of Poppy's wrist and feels for his pulse. He delicately replaces Poppy's hand onto the bed and looks over to me in the shadows of my corner. For some reason he looks suspicious of me. I wonder if it has anything to do with Poppy's increase of Librium. By Poppy's orders I am giving him twice the dosage indicated on the bottle. I'm not sure why he has ordered me to add the extra dosage; at the same time, when considering his physical condition, it seems obvious. I would like to tell the doctor, but it simply isn't my place. As it stands, I am to abide by the rule which states: *Contradictions and illogicalities discovered by staff members are to be ignored and not spoken of unless a formal query is made by Mr. Sherwood, Head of Intelligence, a representative of Mr. Sherwood, or by Mr. Blackwell himself.*

Dr. Barnum's gaze doesn't abate.

I would be more than happy to inform him without compromising myself. However, I don't know how to go about it. I am not clever enough. I am exhausted. I haven't slept in a very long time.

Dr. Barnum, the boys, and I watch the TV.

The closed circuit network scans the floors of the casino. Every nine segments the camera closes in on a man who's full bodied, round faced, well dressed, and unshaven standing at the head of a roulette table in Gaming Room Three. He pinches the bridge of his nose with his fingers each time he lays down ten thousand dollars on a spread of 2, 3, 5, 6, 8, 9, 11, 12, 32, 33, 35, and 36. He doesn't appear to have a system; he just continues to bet the same numbers over and over in different variations of one-number, two-number, and four-number bets. He is losing miserably and as far as I can remember has been at the same table for the past three hours.

Obese women licking ice cream cones and dressed in tight white polo shirts gather around to watch. After a moment, this man's image becomes fixed on the screen. The rotation of the cameras ceases, which means he has reached a certain debt ceiling, the exact amount of which I can't tell. The gold bars of the pay-out/ collection counter glisten behind him.

The television begins to chime loudly.

Poppy's eyes hesitantly flutter open.

The sonorous expression on his face makes me feel groggy.

The croupier, a man with puffy cheeks and chin, is approached by a tuxedo clad pit boss whose thick mustache brushes against the dealer's ear. As these two men whisper to each other, the man gambling reshuffles his new pile of chips once, twice, a third time. The pit boss walks away and the croupier spins the silver ball over the track. Once the ball is released, the man gambling pinches the bridge of his nose, hesitates a moment, and evenly distributes his bets. As the ball orbits the inner wheel, two security guards who have been standing in the background step up and stand directly behind the gambler. They place their hands on his shoulders and the guard on the left of the screen whispers something to him. When the ball slows, drops, and settles into place on number twenty-three, the croupier cleans up the chips and the security guards swivel the man around in his seat. They lift him up and escort him away by his elbows.

Poppy is now fully awake.

He awkwardly bends down to his feet and pulls his blanket up to his waist.

"Dr. Barnum," he says. Poppy's voice is weak, but much stronger than it was earlier. The two bearded men stare at one another and I can feel a silent and strange tension begin to surface on their faces as the hum of the ventilation system changes keys.

"How are you feeling tonight?" Dr. Barnum asks.

"Fine, Felonius. Just fine."

Dr. Barnum reaches for Poppy's wrist to take his pulse again.

"There's no need for that," Poppy admonishes, pulling his hand from the doctor. He sits up, pressing his palms into the mattress.

"No, I imagine not," Dr. Barnum says with an uncharacteristic, nervous smile as he slowly pulls his hands back into his lap and bows his head. His cheeks deflate. After a moment, the doctor lifts his head from his chest as though he has carefully thought through what he wants to say.

"They have begun to talk, H. H."

"Yes, I know. I've heard them."

"They understand the full gravity of the situation."

"So it seems," Poppy contemplates. "You've done a fine job of spreading the word, Felonius."

Poppy and Dr. Barnum's eyes briefly engage each other's and then drift away to different sides of the room. Poppy looks to the two boys standing against the gray wall. Dr. Barnum looks at me but doesn't seem to see me this time.

"Herbert."

"Yes, Felonius."

"Mr. Sherwood and I were hoping you might explain your sudden change of heart."

"I have explained. It has been explained."

"Yes, you're right, of course. But…Mr. Sherwood and I…I mean, consider," Dr. Barnum says, turning back to Poppy. "We've been dedicated! Loyalists from the start! And now…well…in a matter of hours, you've managed to take away everything we worked for, everything you've promised us."

"I've done what I've done for good reason," Poppy says. "I don't expect you to understand. But in all fairness, Felonius, I've given you a decent chance to regain what's yours. I suggest you keep at it. To the end."

"Don't get me wrong. I appreciate your decision to give us the chance you have. But in the end, what value does our life have without the value of what we earned from G.? Why should we even pursue this if the risk is for absolutely nothing?"

"Your chances are good," Poppy assures him. "At this point, it is a matter of will and wit. You do what you do. I'll do as I do. You will see it to the end for the same reason as I. Because the risk *isn't* for absolutely nothing. You know that as well as Mr. Sherwood." Poppy pats down the edge of his blanket with his long fingers. "But there must a parting of the ways."

"I don't accept this," Dr. Barnum says, shaking his head angrily. "You've done this to disgrace us! Plain and simple. To humiliate us! The least you can do, Herbert, is to allow us the dignity to be worthy opponents."

"And how might I do that?"

"By providing us with more information!…about the diagrams we retrieved yesterday from 747 Romaine. Without it, you've left us crippled."

Poppy shakes his head indifferently. "You have what you need. I haven't done anything to disadvantage you."

"Come, H. H.," Dr. Barnum says as he waves to the boys to prepare the diagrams.

"You don't understand, Felonius. You're not going to find what you're looking for here," Poppy says resolutely, holding up his hand to the boys. They obediently halt and return to the wall.

Dr. Barnum smiles with reddened cheeks. "Come, Herbert. For old times' sake then."

"No," Poppy asserts. "You've made a great deal of progress thus far. If you continue your interrogations you'll find what you're looking for."

Dr. Barnum weighs this for a moment. "Please excuse us," he says to the boys. The doctor looks across the room to me, and in a defiant tone says, "You too, Mr. Louse!"

I am deeply confused by this, by the nature of the entire conversation. My body stiffens as Dr. Barnum's glare flattens me against the wall. I look over to Poppy.

"Go ahead, Herman," he says.

"Yes, sir," I say, and step out toward the western wing.

When I step out into the hall, the two boys are already turning the corner into the southern wing. Passing them are Mr. Bender and Mr. Godmeyer. The men's shadows trail along the museum cases whose planes look as if they are hovering in midflight.

I take a few short steps into the hall so that I am out of the path of the two men. As they step into the shaft of light coming from the kitchen, they fix their eyes on me until they reach the door to Poppy's chambers.

"Good evening, Mr. Louse," Mr. Bender says.

"Good evening, Mr. Bender," I say, shaken. "Mr. Godmeyer."

When they reach the end of the wing, they turn into Poppy's chambers and close the door behind them. As the door slams shut, Mr. Lutherford and Mr. Heinrik peek their heads out of the kitchen and step into the hall. The two men remove the masks they are required to wear in "Sterilization," and look down the wing.

Mr. Lutherford waves at me to come toward them. Beside the spindly Mr. Heinrik, Mr. Lutherford looks like a mountain. "Have you heard anything in the wings, Mr. Louse?" Mr. Lutherford inquires.

"Anything at all?" Mr. Heinrik follows.

I shake my head at them. "No, no, nothing, nothing at all," I sputter.

"There is no reason to withhold information, Mr. Louse," Mr. Lutherford follows. "You may discuss these matters freely. We are at liberty, if you recall, to discuss such matters freely."

"I know my rights very well in this regard, Mr. Lutherford. Thank you for your advice and concern."

The two men turn to one another as if to confirm what they believed about me. At this point my neighbor, Mr. Crane, the maintenance engineer, and Ms. Morris, a member of the cleaning crew, a diminutive woman with a squeaky voice who is a little hard of hearing, greet Mr. Lutherford and Mr. Heinrik in the hall. They stand huddled around, speaking confidentially. All with the exception of Ms. Morris.

"No, he never does," Ms. Morris squeaks. She looks up from the group and smiles at me as though I can't hear what she's saying, as though she thinks I can't tell she is talking about me. "But I've just come from Communications. They found out, a moment after, from Pan Opticon." Ms. Morris pauses and looks at me again. "They are saying," she continues, then breaks into inaudible whispers. When she is through with what she has to say, she looks at me again. So does everyone else. No smiles this time. Everyone just looks intent on saying something more. "Yes. Well, you know, you can always trust most of what you hear," Ms. Morris says plainly.

"They've come out with more names," Mr. Crane says, diverting their attention.

"Oh yes?" Mr. Heinrik inquires.

"Fordham, Reynolds, and Olivier," Crane informs.

"Is that right?" Ms. Morris squeaks.

"I believe I've met Reynolds," Mr. Lutherford boasts.

"Olivier…Olivier. I know that one," Heinrik remarks.

"Fordham somehow doesn't surprise me," Crane asserts.

"Nor me," Ms. Morris seconds.

"We all know him," Lutherford proclaims.

"He's been through here, hasn't he?" Ms. Morris queries.

"On more than one occasion," says Crane.

"What does that make it now?" asks Heinrik.

"Fordham, Reynolds…," Crane lists.

"Olivier, Lumpit…," Morris lists.

"Nester, Kovax…," Lutherford adds.

"Blank, mustn't forget Blank! And Berger and Blurd," Heinrik finishes.

"Oh Blurd. Blurd, Blurd, Blurd," Crane says contemplatively.

"No. Blurd doesn't surprise me at all," says Lutherford.

"Imagine. With a name like that…," Ms. Morris says.

"Yes. I've passed that one in the hall," says Crane.

"He likes to hum, that one, doesn't he?" says Heinrik.

"Blurd?" Lutherford blurts.

"Oh yes. Blurd is a hummer," confirms Heinrik.

"I've heard Blurd hum," Ms. Morris says sheepishly.

"It's no wonder a man of such free spirit is under suspicion," denounces Lutherford.

"Have you ever found yourself humming?" Crane intones.

"No. I can't say that I have," Ms. Morris confesses.

"As far as I know I've never been much of a hummer," Heinrik jests.

"Oh, but that Blurd surely is," Lutherford confirms.

"They say Blurd hums nonstop," Ms. Morris announces.

"They are thinking of putting him in isolation," Crane conjectures.

"Sending him to the outer wings," Heinrik elaborates.

"To the under wings," Lutherford embellishes.

"That Blurd!" they all exclaim. "That Blurd!"

"May he find some self control," Ms. Morris snaps. "Some self discipline."

Ms. Morris glimpses over to me. She can't contain herself. Nor can any of them. *Rumors of the accused do not merit truth. Invention for invention's sake is appropriate and encouraged. Fictions cast onto the suspicious enables the authorities of truth to reveal more truth.* Ms. Morris giggles. She and then the rest.

"That Blurd must have a strong reprimand coming to him," Lutherford announces.

"He must have already lost his privileges to Paradise."

"At least bumped back on the list."

"Bumped completely, I'd say."

"Oh, no doubt," they say. "No doubt."

They all stare gravely as though they have moved the conversation a little beyond the boundaries they are allowed. *To speak of Paradise in vain is a punishable offense.* I feel great pleasure as Ms. Morris raises her hand to her mouth and as Mr. Crane bites down on his lower lip. Lutherford has cast his eyes to the floor. Mr. Heinrik, as well. However, Mr. Heinrik slowly lifts his eyes and looks at me, suddenly possessed with a new spirit. "Oh, that Blurd," he says and lets out a short staccato giggle. The giggle distracts everyone from their contemplation and infects them with a little humor. They look at each other. "Yes, that Blurd," they say, one after the other, and the giggles grow louder until they all simultaneously wilt into expressions of discomfort.

Mr. Heinrik and Mr. Lutherford, without bidding anyone good-bye or good fortune bow their heads and silently turn back into the kitchen. Ms. Morris and Mr. Crane follow.

I remain standing alone beside the entryway to Poppy's chambers.

As I lean against the wall, for some inexplicable reason I can hear voices drifting through the intercom next to the door. They are soft, but clear, and when I stand still I can hear each and every utterance. Considering that this is my position for the time being, and there is none other I can think of to go to, I stand at attention.

"Your bravado is unnecessary, gentlemen," Poppy says.

"You still don't fully understand our position." It is Mr. Sherwood. His voice is stern and unforgiving and twice as loud as the others—perhaps because he is speaking to them from his office over the intercom.

"You'll simply have to be more clever, Mr. Sherwood. I told you there are many doors and many passages, many dead ends. Track down the money and it's yours. If you don't find it, you will lose it. How can I be more fair?"

"You're playing games," Dr. Barnum insists. "Games in which you have the advantage and games meant to distract us."

"But it is a game," Poppy insists. "It's a game of devices and deceits. But other than that, it's not a game at all. It's deadly serious,

Felonius. There is one last thing that I wish to accomplish. I believe you're in my way of accomplishing it, and therefore, I must either surrender my vision on your behalf or push you aside to obtain it. It's as simple as that. Yet, I'm willing to play it out, gentlemen. Just to show you that it is nothing personal. I respect the loyalty you've shown me all these years. In fact, I cherish it enough to give you a fighting chance."

"Our intent has never been to obstruct your ambition, Herbert," Mr. Sherwood says.

"I've seen your objections to my plans, Mr. Sherwood. I have read them carefully and know with what intent they were drawn."

"You'll excuse me, but I've had enough of this," Mr. Bender breaks in. "Let's just get this over with. You two act as though there is some chivalry involved in this."

"Shut your mouth, Mr. Bender," Mr. Sherwood orders.

"This is ridiculous. There's no reasoning with him," Mr. Bender continues on defiantly. "You act as though he is going to give us what you want on his own free will. He is stubborn, more stubborn than you."

"I think the young man is correct in his assessment, Mr. Sherwood," Poppy replies. "You two would do well to listen to the younger ones."

"We should be rid of him once and for all," Mr. Bender continues.

"Yes, very clever, Mr. Bender. I like your style," Poppy declares. "You have chosen well, Mr. Sherwood."

"But really, Herbert, what's keeping us from it?" the doctor asks.

"I don't know. You seem ready for the worst of all outcomes. This one you could be sure of."

"Please, H. H.," Mr. Sherwood intones.

"What is it you're afraid of?" Mr. Bender demands.

A moment of silence passes.

"He claims that if we were to harm him, the Head Engineer can and will destroy G. and Paradise as well. We believe he has a cache of explosives to do as he says."

Mr. Bender doesn't say anything at first.

"It's a bluff," he finally asserts. "If he destroys G. and Paradise, he will destroy everything."

"Look at him," Dr. Barnum says.

"Yes, look at me, Mr. Bender," Poppy says.

Another moment of silence passes.

Mr. Bender is speechless.

"And now that's he's managed to launder the accumulated wealth of G. from our accounts into his private coffers, he'll have his vision," Mr. Sherwood surrenders.

"Paradise Beyond Paradise…," Dr. Barnum broods.

"Wasn't Paradise enough for you?" Mr. Sherwood asks.

"No," Poppy says. "It wasn't Paradise enough."

"I've had it," Mr. Bender declares somewhat more timidly than before.

"Enough," Mr. Sherwood affirms.

"Enough," Dr. Barnum agrees.

And with that the voices disappear as mysteriously as they appeared. I lean my head toward the door to see if I can hear anything else. But the hall is perfectly still. Some sounds drift from the kitchen where I can hear Ms. Lonesome cleaning something in the sink. And then suddenly, the door to Poppy's chambers opens. Mr. Bender, Dr. Barnum, and Mr. Godmeyer exit and storm down the wing in the same manner that they arrived.

RADISE – DEC

Dear Members of the Board of Directors:

We, Homo sapiens, rule the world. We rule by destroying that within the reach of our hands to create the unreal illusion of our destinies. In part, this is because our brains in proportion to our bodies are large and are growing ever larger to parallel the exponential rate of our expanded consciousness. Our instincts, more than any other creature's, more than in any other time, are becoming fashioned in the shape of what we once defined as God's. Though we may be in the form of animals, die like animals, decay like animals, we are no longer animals in thought. Only when we remind ourselves. Millions of years of an evolutionary fallacy have shaped us into creatures who grow in concordance with belief as opposed to necessity, therefore, disassociating our consciousness from our physicality. Primarily, our belief has been in our inner selves, in what we perceive, and not in those invisible external forces that shape us. Yes, it is true, that we react when darkness envelops us, when fear grips our imaginations, causing us to grunt, howl, and shriek like the presyllabic animals that we once were. However, when the danger is gone we return to our cages and revel in the reflections of our human form, forgetting the intermittent threats of the bygone wilds; instead, we believe in the peace of restful moments and ignore the involuntary movements of our bodies—breathing, blinking, beating—and don't look to see the microscopic life that sinks into our pores and hangs on the end of every strand of hair. The invisible is masked by dreams of larger forms and by convincing ourselves of our species' immortality. We dream to survive and sublimate our desires into compulsive acts that we don't even see when they are happening. They pass us by like the mist and ooze of the primordial earth we arose from; we shock ourselves with repetitive actions to simulate the sensation of the chase or of being chased by animals across open fields, the entire time daydreaming of ephemeral things such as love and wealth and beauty.

We have dropped from the trees. We dropped our prehensile tails, stood upright to walk the plains and run through fields. We put our hands to air, fire, and water and the remainder of the material universe to make a simple equation of everything that we once thought of as magic. We laboriously thought through our dilemmas and applied reason; we designed, constructed. We split from the sensual to the divine as our tools grew more complex and evolution spired into paragons of reason. The concept of time became defined relative to the subject and no longer applied to the universe as a constant. Time for a man became relative to that of a lion. Time for a lion became relative to that of a beetle. Time for a beetle became relative to that of bacteria. Time for bacteria became relative to that of a quasar. We have come to exist one next to the other, as equals regardless of species or purpose, and all of our complexity that we once thought of as divine has temporarily brought us to crisis. We have become closer to the truth of our ephemerality. We have learned that stars die and collapse, that universes may be numerous, or multiply, that holes spiral through the vacuum of space, that human life is not as precious as it might seem, that it may take on many forms all throughout the galaxies. There is, therefore, nothing particularly special about man and woman, other than that they exist for the time being as an entity equal to that of a dust mite, who perceives a crop of hair as an ocean of immortality which infinite generations will occupy. When all the knowledge is weighed from the data we collect what's left is the cruel acknowledgment that we are not immortal and never will be. But yet this is still our greatest desire—to procreate until we perpetuate ourselves throughout infinity.

I will say it bluntly. Before the sun ever ebbs into its final decline, we will have done, we will believe we have conquered, and then we will ultimately fail. For we are too complex. The fact of the matter is that bacteria, being one of the simplest forms of life and the most nefarious infidel, will have destroyed us. They are simple. They carry with them the map of life, from which anything can grow. We, in our human form, therefore, are merely intermediaries, experiments of this life, that for a brief moment in time will allow these pests to carry their mission of survival forward. As I have said, the smaller the creature, the better likelihood of survival, anywhere, anytime. Consider that there are only four thousand species of mammals, whereas in the insect world there are five hundred thousand species of beetles alone! There is no telling what the single celled creatures are capable of. Not to mention the inanimate nature of any single virus, suspended in its state of unnatural perpetuity! It is a nightmare for me to imagine any of these invisible creatures. They are devious little pests who, if not persistently challenged and battled, or simply avoided, will take over on their wits alone.

Thus we are left with a great dilemma: As long as there is life, as long as there is a sun in the sky and a moon above Earth, bacteria and viruses will always be here to use us as their vehicle for survival, do as they will, and thrive beyond us. They occupy the bodies of the mites that occupy our bodies. They deliver disease and pestilence that leaches life from our veins. They can live with or without direct sun light, with or without oxygen. All they need is a vital energy source to feed from and they are able to sustain the most fundamental existence. Our decision, therefore, pertains to our desire to perpetuate a life form that wreaks such havoc on us. It is my belief that as much as we try to avoid them we cannot. But it is my intent to try.

It goes without saying that all solutions are no solutions to rid ourselves of such a foe. Any technological solutions we employ to solve our problems must retain their logic. This, of course, is an impossibility. We are therefore faced with a determined paradox: to perpetuate human life for human life's sake or to perpetuate life (bacterial/viral life) at the expense of human life.

If my common sense is the purveyor of wisdom, I believe we should abandon the very source of life in order to dissect the contradictions inherent in this problem. I have therefore begun construction of a sanctuary for a select group of individuals. I have used a great deal of my fortune to gather the technologies and the resources, to make plans and designs to transport us to a place where we will hopefully become free from our servitude. Our futures will be built on the backs of all the hardworking men and women whose debt to us is being repaid by sacrificing their lives for this worthy cause. I offer no apologies to those who sacrifice unwillingly. If I have been a tyrant, let them say so. May they write epic poems about me as Pushkin wrote of Russia's Peter the Great. I will be proud to be a Bronze Horseman chasing young delirious clerks around my gift to humanity. Let them say one day,

> Centuries passed, and there shone forth
> From the abyss of a vacant prism,
> Crown gem and marvel of the heavens,
> The proud young city newly risen.
> Where the debauched before,
> Harsh cosmos' wretched waif, were plying,
> Forlorn beyond any fallow field,
> Their fates, with brittle wills trying

Uncharted scores — now bustling,
Standing serried in well-ordered ranks
Of palaces and towers; converging
From the four corners of the earth,
Sails soaring to seek the opulent berths

…and so on…

I will be the first inhabitant, as Peter was in his grand Winter Palace with his window onto the West. I will stand guard in my chambers as the rest of the world huddles in fear. I will ride in my ship to the landing docks and will rest comfortably in my chambers where nothing lives other than me and those fortunate enough to share in my experience.

We will not be eaten by germs!

This will be my legacy!

Yours sincerely,
Herbert Horatio Blackwell
Executive Controlling Partner

8. THE MIDNIGHT MOVIE

HE MIDNIGHT

When I enter Poppy's chambers he is doubled over, coughing deep from within his chest. "Mr. Louse," he says between coughs, "please uncap my bottle of NeHi."

I obey his command. I walk to the eastern night table and uncap the bottle of grape NeHi with my opener and replace the beverage on the night table. When his coughing subsides, Poppy picks it up and drinks. He cranes his neck so that I can see the wedged ashen rings under his eyes. He replaces the bottle on the night table as he breathes a shallow breath.

"I'm ready, Mr. Louse."

"Yes, sir."

Eighteen feet beyond the TV is a closet. I open the door and remove Poppy's gurney, on top of which is a sterile sheet, a freshly laundered hospital gown, a mask, and a pair of latex gloves—all sealed together in a plastic bag. I wheel the gurney over the papers and the Kleenex so that it is a few feet from the edge of the bed. I remove the gown, mask, and gloves from the bag and dress myself in all these garments. Once dressed I remove the sterile sheet from the bag, place the bag in the pocket of my hospital gown, and spread the sheet over the gurney. I then turn to Poppy and prepare to lift him. He closes his eyes as I dig my arms under his upper thighs and upper back and—feeling acutely aware of his brittle hips, shoulders, and neck—I lift his body in one clean jerk. He growls a little. He continues growling as I quickly turn around and delicately lower and arrange his body so that it is straight and flat on the gurney.

"All right," he says, pointing ahead.

"Yes, sir," I say.

I look ahead, over his body, as I push him forward. He is silent during our trip. All I can hear are his toe nails and finger nails clattering against each other as I slightly jostle the cart with each step.

I'm unsure of what to make of what's happening. There has no doubt been a breach of contract. On whose shoulders this rests seems impossible to say. However, if this schism didn't involve Poppy and if the stakes weren't so high, it would seem like any other night in G. There are always arrests, interrogations, rumors about so-and-so who did this or that. A few details are divulged and the consequences are reported. In the past, no one seems to have been above these proceedings, other than Poppy, Dr. Barnum, and Mr. Sherwood. Mr. Kreslin, for instance, the man who was replaced by Mr. Bender, was arrested, viewed, and disposed of to one of the higher floors in a position no one has knowledge of. But to have Poppy being accused by Dr. Barnum and Mr. Sherwood is highly irregular. And to have Poppy reprimanding and manipulating Dr. Barnum and Mr. Sherwood is equally irregular; as a rule they have always reprimanded and manipulated other offenders together.

I roll Poppy's gurney onto the tiled floor and pull up to the toilet. Poppy begins humming the third movement of Mozart's

"Requiem" to himself and slowly rocks his head back and forth to the brooding tempo. Putting one hand behind his fragile head and one hand on his back, I lift him. He manages to hold himself up on his own as I swing his legs around and grab his feet before they can drop to the floor. He continues humming as I undress him of his diaper. I stand facing him and lift him with one hand under his legs and the other on his lower back. I bend forward, then lift him with his waist securely over my shoulder. I approach the toilet with my head pointing into the ring of water reflecting the old man's bottom, and I rest him comfortably on his throne.

I stand in the southwest corner of the bathroom as Poppy watches EKG Production *H.A. 13-3*. The lights are lowered. A green glow emanates from Jane's holographic image on the medicine cabinet. Flashes of black and white illuminate and shade Poppy's naked body, his corrugated ribs and chest, his stick-thin arms and scabrous feet, planted on the tiles like broken urns. He dips forward on his arm rests, barely able to hold himself up, and stares mercifully at the screen as Monte (played by the young Ronald Sherwood) and Roy Ruteledge (played by a vibrant young Poppy), brothers and fellow Oxford students, prepare for battle. They don ascots, goggles, and leather flight jackets embossed with Royal Flying Corps patches on the breasts and arms. They are running through cobblestone streets to the outskirts of the city.

The year is 1914.

The camera cuts to Karl Arnstedt. The Kaiser has just sent a zeppelin to bomb London. On board is Karl, a former Oxford student who is friendly with both Monte and Roy. He has only recently left Britain out of duty to fight for his fatherland even though his heart belongs to the green pastures of England and the hallowed halls of his college.

The immense airship silently glides through the night and comes to a stop over a low-lying London fog. As the zeppelin hovers in miniature against the dark starry sky, the maniacal and monocled commander of the ship fastens Karl to a harness attached to a steel cable and lowers him out the zeppelin's belly. When he descends below the clouds, Karl realizes he is the only one who could possibly know the outcome of the bombing. Acting out of desperate uncertainty, he sends a premature communication to his commander, which results in all the bombs landing harmlessly in the Thames. The commander, convinced that he has just obliterated Trafalgar Square, delightedly orders the zeppelin to return home.

However, the commander's countenance quickly changes when four British fighter planes—two of which are piloted by the Ruteledge brothers—rise out of the fog bank. Suddenly desperate to make a fast retreat, the commander disengages the cable from which Karl is hanging, sending him to his death. He orders all equipment thrown overboard, and then orders half his crew overboard as well. One after the other the airmen, "Fur Kaiser und Vaterland," do as ordered. A short battle ensues, during which three of the British planes—including the Ruteledge brothers'—are damaged and must break formation to return to base. The remaining pilot, however, sacrifices his life by crashing into the zeppelin, causing it to burst into flames.

Poppy narcotically nods at this with pleasure.

I have seen this film a dozen times as of tonight. I find myself unable to concentrate on its presence as I watch the zeppelin burn. I think of Karl Arnstedt plummeting to his death. His arms stretch out like those of an angel as he careens head first toward the docks. Each movement and line of his body precipitates my mind to wander through the patterns of the story. My thoughts reel forward to the French canteens and the barracks where images of Roy and Monte's laughing faces, Poppy and Mr. Sherwood's faces, mock the jeopardy they are about to put themselves in. I imagine the British General addressing the pilots, explaining that the Allied attack cannot be successful unless the German munitions depot is destroyed. Poppy and Mr. Sherwood silently ride a train through the mountains to an airfield where they board a captured German Gotha. Before they can get to the Gotha in my mind, I flash back onto the train and see the blur of the passing landscape from Monte's point of view. I can hear the *tuh-tuh-tuh tuh-tuh-tuh* rotation of the wheels, and suddenly can see myself in the window again. The image alternates between myself and Mr. Sherwood. The melody I hummed in the study momentarily returns to my mind. I don't hum it. I just listen to it, trying to fit it into the scheme of the film, wondering if this is where it comes from, if it is a melody I have simply forgotten, if this is possible. And then the image of the window is no longer the window of the train; it has been elevated to the height of a mountain and shows me the same scene I remember seeing in my mind in Poppy's study. I can see the image of myself reflected in the window, the dark figure behind me and a new, unrecognizable figure behind that. And then they are there and gone, and I am gone, and all I can see now are images from the rest of the movie.

The German Gotha flies into enemy territory where Monte and Roy successfully annihilate the target. The battle music rises to a crescendo of bassoons, French horns, and flutes, until the

Ruteledge brothers begin their return trip, at which time the bassoons and French horns are joined with accents of contemplative oboe, and the triumph descends into doom as the score drones into the sounds of propellers cutting the wind. The bombing has been observed by Baron Manfred von Richthofen whose theme is ominously rich with pounding timpani that, even in memory, rumbles my chest, and transports my thoughts to the Allied planes engaging in fierce dogfights with the Germans. The music rises to a new crescendo with strings and volleys of machine gun fire all the way up to the point that the Gotha is shot down. And then the sound track goes silent. All we can hear is the rush of wind on the wings and the drone, not of propellers this time, but of plummeting descent.

The rest is drama. The music fades into the back of my thoughts and I can't hear anything. When captured, the brothers are tortured as they are questioned about the expected Allied push. Monte, unable to endure Baron von Kranz's brutality any longer, agrees to tell what he knows in order to save his life. Poppy also agrees, but it's a trick; in exchange for the battle plans, Poppy asks for and is given a pistol with a single bullet in order to cleanse his shame. Instead he shoots his brother, who when breathing his last breath says, "Don't cry, it was the only thing you could do!" Moments later, Poppy stands before of a firing squad and cries, "I'll be with you in just a moment, Monte!" As the last bit of smoke rises from the German gun barrels, the mist rises from the trenches along the devastated landscape of the Western Front. All of a sudden, with cheers and wails, long lines of soldiers emerge from their holes and forge their way onto the enemy's line.

My eyes feel so heavy and I can't place this melody that runs through my head. Maybe it has to do with the fact that I haven't slept in such a very long time now, so long I don't remember the last time. The time I did sleep, it couldn't have been for more than a few hours, and that time I remember I didn't even really fall asleep. I was so nervous, nervous Poppy would call and I wouldn't hear him. I closed my eyes in anticipation of hearing his voice come over the intercom in my room calling, "Herman Q. Louse!" Over and over, in my mind, I could see him watching me sleep as he called. Even seeing how exhausted I was he still called, not giving up, not calling any other attendant, but me. "Herman Q. Louse!" is all I heard that night as I drifted through auditory phantoms. Hours passed with my eyes closed as my mind traced shadows onto darkness. I counted thousands forward and back, thinking many thoughts at once. His voice swelled and infected the room. I could even smell him.

I must think quick thoughts now, little jabs, like needles he supplies me with.

...three inches long to stick in my palms at the base of each finger, to keep me from sleeping, keep me aware. *No stimulants...*pure attendants only...*needles to be kept in shirt pockets to stick in palms of hand...*

...*if boredom reigns and brings on sleep, induce pain...*

Take my pins to hand now, in order to save myself from further humiliation...from sleep...here, standing beside him...face the television...

It's unheard of, this...

...planes fighting over Western Front...men throwing themselves onto grenades...

...try to see the movie from another perspective...

...all blurs together...

…afraid I'm done for…

…already see his eyes before me…

…Mr. Louse…

…Mr. Louse…

…Mr. Louse…

…Mr. Louse…

…Mr. Louse…

…Mr. Louse…

"Yes," I say, shaken to complete and total awareness.

I am no longer standing. Mr. Slodsky, Poppy's second ward, is standing over me, upside down. We are in motion. His bald head bobs to and fro. A rather skinny man with a pockmarked face, Mr. Slodsky incessantly stoops his shoulders. He has a nervous twitch in his left cheek that mostly twitches when he stutters, but occasionally twitches when he steps down onto his right foot at a particular angle. Other than the stooped shoulders, the pockmarks, and the twitch, he is a handsome man. He has a square jaw, which is nicely proportioned with his nose and brow. His gray eyes complement our blue ties. He has large arms and legs and perfect teeth. Mr. Slodsky's fresh scent of ammonia wafts deep into my lungs.

"G-G-Good evening, Mr. Louse," Mr. Slodsky stutters. His facial tic spasms just above the left corner of his mouth. The dragging motion slightly slurs his speech.

"Good evening, Mr. Slodsky. Where am I?"

"You f-f-fainted."

"Fainted?" I ask. I feel particularly nauseated and my head feels heavy.

"Yes, f-f-fainted."

"Where am I?"

"On Mr. Blackwell's gurney. North wing. Twenty-first floor."

"Where are we going?"

"To Lounge Eighteen SR-Five."

"I don't understand."

"I have exp-p-press instructions from M-M-M-Mr. Blackwell that you b-b-be treated."

"Oh?"

"S-s-s-see for yourself."

Mr. Slodsky reaches into his inside jacket pocket and removes a manila envelope.

He hands it to me.

I open it.

Mr. Louse:

I am concerned with your health. It has been brought to my attention that in addition to falling asleep during the midnight movie, you were caught displaying an act of free will while performing your duties in the study. I know that, as a result, you have been fined in accordance with the severity of your transgression. Because you are my ward and I am your guardian, I wish to have all such incidents avoided in the future. I have, therefore, in what I deem as a preventative measure, made arrangements for you in Lounge 18 SR-5. In order to allow your more primitive predilections to be expunged, I encourage you, on a regular basis, to physically act out these anxieties and have them done away with once and for all. I thus order you to initiate this process by arriving at Lounge 18 SR-5, Floor 21, upon receipt of this correspondence.

Your Devoted Guardian,

Herbert Horatio Blackwell

Executive Controlling Partner

"Did Poppy indicate it was necessary to take me all the way if I were awake?" I ask.

"He p-p-placed no c-c-conditions on my orders."

"Would you mind stopping then?"

"It's only a sh-sh-short distance, Mr. Louse. I don't m-m-mind. And b-b-besides, you don't look very good."

"But really, Mr. Slodsky…"

"Really," he says, "it's n-n-no trouble, n-n-no trouble at all."

Mr. Slodsky's eyes shut when he stutters. They stretch into narrow ovals as though his pupils have momentarily disappeared. When he opens them they turn into the back of his head in search of the proper consonant and the serenity to finish his sentence.

"Some n-n-new news has been reported since you've been asleep, M-M-Mr. Louse."

"Is that so?" I say, feeling a little fuzzy about the old news. I try to recall what has happened, but all I can think of is Karl Arnstedt falling to his death.

We pass a number of tinted glass doors to the left of us. To the right is a wall lined with photographs of missiles and rocket ships lifting off launch platforms, flying into colorful halos.

"You're n-n-never interested in the news, are you?" Mr. Slodsky persists.

"That's not true, Mr. Slodsky," I protest, feeling some blood rush to my face. "I listen and report what I know when asked."

Mr. Slodsky clears his throat. "I imagine that is all we are expected t-t-to do."

"Yes, Mr. Slodsky. I…"

"But don't you think it worthwhile—to pay closer attention?" he asks. "For your—benefit? For all of our—benefits?"

"What are you trying to say, Mr. Slodsky?"

"I'm not trying to ins-s-s-sinuate anything, Mr. Louse. This is s-s-s-simply a matter of conjecture, seeing that you're there and I'm here…s-s-s-since it's allowed to th-th-th-theorize about such personal m-m-matters."

"I'll have you know, Mr. Slodsky, I can recite all that I hear on any given night with great accuracy *and* clarity of speech."

"I don't d-d-d-doubt that, Mr. Louse," he says, his voice quavering and his eyes blinking nervously. He looks into my upside-down eyes and then looks up toward the end of the corridor. "I don't d-d-d-doubt that, Mr. Louse," he repeats. After a few steps, he looks down at me as though I have injured him.

I didn't mean to. I wasn't thinking of what I was saying. "Yes," I say, contemplating what I just did.

"I just w-w-wonder about your w-w-willingness t-to d-do so. You s-s-s-simply seem unw-w-w-willing," he pursues. Mr. Slodsky's tic freezes into what I see as an attempt at a placating smile.

"Yes, I can see that, Mr. Slodsky."

"Yes, w-w-well, in any case, Mr. Louse," Mr. Slodsky continues, not giving up. "Since you're th-there and I'm here, I don't im-m-magine you would mind if I told you what I know. Compare n-n-notes. That kind of thing."

"Of course not," I say. "It is my duty, after all."

"I thought you might—see it as such," he says excitedly, as though he has finally captured a willing participant to listen through his pauses.

I surrender a smile in the direction of Mr. Slodsky's cleft chin. "Go on, Mr. Slodsky. Please."

"Well, it turns out that M-M-Ms. Berger…You know Ms. Berger?"

"I recall hearing talk of her."

"V-v-very g-g-good. It turns out th-th-that…uhm, they discovered a host of notes in Ms. Berger's desk from M-M-Mr. M-M-Moorcraft."

"The Head Engineer."

"Precisely," Mr. Slodsky punctuates. He tightens and then relaxes his face into a meditative mask. As he looks deeply into the back of his head for some calm, I begin to think of Mr. Moorcraft's threat. "M-M-Mr. Moorcraft," Mr. Slodsky continues slowly, looking very serious now, "of course, denies any wrong doing. P-P-Pan Opticon is checking into his s-s-statements. But it is r-r-rumored that he has had connections with some of the others."

"The others?" I question. "Which others?"

"The others!" Mr. Slodsky exclaims. "W-w-why M-M-Mr. Blank, for instance. Sh-sh-surely you've heard of M-M-Mr. Blank by now?"

"Yes, of course," I say.

"Of c-c-course you have," Mr. Slodsky says with his naked brow raised. The camera surveillance lights mounted on the ceiling streak past his head like a swarm of fire flies. "Yes, of course," he continues. "W-w-well, M-M-Mr. Louse, it has been reported that correspondence from M-M-Mr. Blank to the Head Engineer has b-b-been d-d-discovered in a trunk on the thirtieth floor. But this, for the record, Mr. Louse, is only rumor and not considered information yet."

"I understand, Mr. Slodsky."

"In-n-n-in any case, M-M-Mr. Louse," he continues with the same awkward cadence, "Ms. B-B-Berger's detention has b-b-been made public. Mr. M-M-Moorcraft, M-M-Mr. Blank, and the others will be n-n-next, I think."

"Others?"

"Th-th-the others, M-M-Mr. Louse. A-c-c-countants. L-l-launderers. C-c-conspirators. K-K-Kovax, Nestor, and Blurd, to name a few."

"Yes, those," I say.

"W-w-we must remain alert, Mr. Louse."

"Yes, Mr. Slodsky. I agree."

"There could be one hidden b-b-behind every door."

"Yes, Mr. Slodsky."

"Guilty by design."

"Yes, guilty by design."

"Y-y-yes."

"Yes," I say.

"Well, so m-m-much for the news, M-M-Mr. Louse."

"So much for it, Mr. Slodsky."

And with that, Mr. Slodsky stops walking. We have arrived at Lounge 18 SR-5.

"Thank you, Mr. Slodsky," I say as I sit up.

"G-g-good fortune to you, Mr. Louse."

"Good fortune to you, Mr. Slodsky."

I step off the gurney, feeling dizzy and not sure of my legs. Mr. Slodsky does a U-turn and wheels away. I lean against the wall, wait for the wing to stop spinning, and step into the lounge.

The lights here are as dim as the hallway's and the air is warm. There are five leather easy chairs to the left of me and five doors with small green lights attached to the knobs to the right of me. I walk past all to the desk in the back.

"Welcome to Lounge Eighteen," a slender woman behind the desk greets me with a smooth, hushed voice. She is dressed in a low-cut blouse. Her chest rises into two soft mounds of flesh. "Mister...?"

"Mr. Louse," I say as I hand her my identification card.

"Yes, Mr. Louse," she says, taking my ID and looking down at a roster. "You're expected."

The woman smiles at me.

"You may take a seat."

"Yes. Thank you," I say. "Thank you very much."

I turn around and walk over to the seats.

There is only one other man in the room. He is sitting in seat number two with his head resting on the palm of his hand. His eyes are closed and his shoes are untied. As I sit down, I look at the woman again and thankfully nod my head; she looks back at me and smiles. She then looks down at her paperwork.

I untie my shoes, nestle into the comfort of the leather chair, and close my eyes.

When I open them I realize that I have drifted off to sleep for a short moment and dreamed of performing a *quality of life assignment*.

The man beside me is still resting on his palm, but his eyes are open. He turns toward me slightly and I can see they are a rich brown. One pupil is somewhat lazy and drifts toward his nose.

The man nods his head and closes his eyes.

If only my mind were clearer, if I weren't so exhausted, I could have saved myself from fainting. If I were more acute I would have practiced a quality of life assignment. For Poppy wholeheartedly approves of my touching things up, cleaning and reordering, as long as my actions comply with his rules. Anything I can do that might improve his surroundings is considered tolerable behavior. He regularly updates the lists of acceptable activities. I could, for instance, have wiped down the holograms in the bathrooms with lint-free cloth. He approves of cleaning any form of grout or mortar with Q-tips. One swipe here, one swipe there. I am allowed to get on my hands and knees. I have been known to take on this task when I am in need of a break from standing. It is something like this that I could have been doing before I lost concentration and fainted on the job. If I had taken on a quality of life assignment I would have undoubtedly kept myself from dropping off the way I did. With a simple Q-tip, or for that matter, a toothpick, I could have avoided the entire ordeal. A toothpick! Even in the midst of movies, he will take enjoyment from watching me run a toothpick along the seam of two tiles. He likes it when I gather the dirt in its entirety, and place it in a small plastic tube so that he might see it. He marvels at it for a moment and then asks me to store it in a special chest in the supply closet.

Quality of life is a two way street, Poppy has written. I didn't think about it in such terms earlier. I resorted to the measure of last resort—the needles. Needles, however, are hardly practical. Needles are considered to be very high risk, hardly a conservative panacea for my condition. Needles should be used when boredom and exhaustion become interchangeable. They are used to induce pain. But pain alone will not result in alertness. Prescribed with needles is work, any form of quality of life assignment. With work, the pain stimulates an awakening in the heart that blossoms into a second wind—into true alertness. It isn't so much that I didn't have a feeling I should have been practicing quality of life. I felt it somewhere, sublimated. It was just too late. I didn't think of it. It probably could be argued that I am guilty for not being disciplined. Perhaps it can easily be concluded that I deserve whatever punishment awaits me. All I know is that in the future should I ever be as exhausted as I was tonight, I will never resort to needles alone. I will turn to any kind of work, anything within Poppy's reason to keep me moving to the end of my shift.

"You may go in now, Mr. Louse," the woman behind the desk says, her voice soothing me.

I notice that the green light on door number five is shining.

"Thank you," I say.

I get up from my chair and go to the door. I open it and close it behind me. Behind the door is a small white tiled room with a shower, an armoire, and a toilet. I open the armoire and place my shoes and socks at the bottom. I remove the remainder of my clothes and hang them up. I then go into the shower stall, turn on the water, and carefully scrub myself with a washcloth—my hands, my face, my underarms, and genitals. When I am done I throw the washcloth down an incineration chute beside the toilet and walk behind a red velvet curtain opposite the door I walked in from. Behind the curtain is another door which revolves. I spin through to the other side into pitch blackness.

The room is silent.

"Are you here?" I ask, as is customary.

"I'm on the mat below," the voice of the woman whispers.

I crouch to my hands and knees. The floor is made of a thick rubber; the walls are padded; the air is damp, much warmer than the entry hall, and it is slightly scented with an infusion of lilac mist.

"Come," the woman's voice says. "Come sit beside me."

"I'm coming," I whisper.

I gently reach my hand out. I crawl forward until I find her. I touch her side and momentarily hold onto a small fold of her flesh. She reaches up, grips my hand and guides me next to her.

"Will you hold me?" she asks.

"Of course," I say.

"I like to be held for a while," she says, her lips close to my ear.

"That's fine," I say.

I lie down on my back and pull her close to me. She rests her head on my chest and her arm across my stomach. I then feel her thigh cross mine; her ankle brushes down the hair on my shin.

Her body is soft and lean, her skin smooth; her hair falls onto my cheek. I take hold of the arm on my stomach and guide it up to my ribs. I can feel the pulse of her body. It is slow and calm.

"That's nice," she whispers as I stroke her back.

Sex, Poppy has written into the contract, *is a necessary biological function to curtail unnecessary acts of aggression. Sex is to be enjoyed if for no other reason that one cannot curtail one's aggressiveness without the immediate gratification the sex act requires. Orgasm is a means to this end. Enjoyment is, therefore, a necessity and a must. However, this principle is only effective if the sex act is enacted anonymously. If done with an intimate other, it can only lead to delusions of physically possessing one's partner, which can only result in petty jealousies brought on by an innate territorialism, which can only result in an act of aggression. The sex act, therefore, must remain purely sensory and unemotional.*

She gently pulls her arm from my stomach and tickles the inside of my thigh with her nails. With this motion of her hand, I become aroused. My erection lifts away from my body and slowly rises until it bumps against her elbow.

"Don't move," she says.

She lifts her weight off me and disappears into the darkness.

The next thing I know I can feel her clutching my ankles and sweeping her hair over my toes. She lifts my legs and pulls my feet into her two small breasts, the nipples of which are hard and taut. She then pulls my feet down to the soft pouch of her belly. She parts my knees and crawls inside the V until she's far enough along to straddle my hips.

"How do you like it?" she asks.

"I like it just fine."

I can feel the warmth of breath return to my ear, her torso on my stomach, her vagina near my penis.

It is my opinion, Poppy has written, *that Darwin's theory regarding the survival of the fittest is suited not just in relationship to interspecies warfare battling for possession of the Earth, but for intraspecies warfare battling for possession of the Earth.*

She reaches her right hand through her legs and takes hold of my erection. She pulls it up by the base so she can use the head to part her labia. She moistens the tip with her wetness and draws it to the hard nub of her clitoris.

I reach out and take hold of her hips, holding her weight so she can maneuver more easily. And with this done, she slips me inside and grips me tight with a slight quiver. She bends forward and places her chest on mine, arms extended over my shoulders, breasts pressed firmly against my clavicle. I raise my ass off the mat and allow her to use me as she likes. She digs her fingers into the back of my head to gain leverage. She pushes the weight of her ass onto my penis, so hard that my penis bends backwards.

Her motion is slow and rhythmic. I guide her with my hands; I run them from her hips to her ass as she rises and falls.

It is increasingly apparent that as interspecies battles have declined and intraspecies battles have increased, man's urge to possess his counterpart has naturally grown more determined.

"Oh," she whispers in my ear.

I moan for her.

"Oh," she says again.

I moan for her some more.

I push her ass onto my penis so I can feel it more.

"Oh," she groans.

"Oh," I groan.

And as if off the wave of my exclamation, she rises off my chest.

Anonymous procreation, therefore, is a necessary deterrence to maintain the status quo...

I let go of her hips and take hold of her breasts, dimpling and squeezing her nipples with my fists. She squeezes my nipples; I tighten my grip. She twists mine; I twist hers. She grabs the back of my ear with her finger nails, and with that she begins to come. And with that, so do I.

She shrieks.

I moan.

She shrieks some more.

I moan some more.

And for whatever reason, we both begin to weep a little.

And then we become silent.

My penis is still inside her, throbbing against her weight, but it's shrinking and I can feel my sperm seeping out of her and all over my groin.

"Stay there a moment," she says. "Don't move."

She pulls herself away. Meanwhile, I allow myself to enjoy the warmth of my ejaculate in my pubic hair; I touch it with my fingers and bring it up to my nose.

She returns and says, "Hold me a moment longer."

"Of course," I say.

She takes hold of me; and when she does, I feel her slip something between my thighs.

I reach down to feel what she's doing.

"Be careful," she says playfully.

I touch carefully and can feel she's attached something to my leg.

"Just be gentle," she says.

"What is this?" I say.

"A little something to remember me by." She giggles.

"I don't understand," I say and then stop myself from saying more, for I'm afraid of saying too much of anything that could be held against me.

"Will you think of me when you go back to your quarters?" she whispers as she taps the thing she's attached to my inner thigh.

"Yes, of course," I say.

"As you should."

"What is happening?"

"Good-bye," she says moving away from me.

"Good-bye," I say, thinking I should hold onto her until I can get an answer as to what this all means.

"It was a pleasure," she says from a distance.

"It was a pleasure," I say, hearing her door revolve back to the other side, as I feel the thing between my legs. It is slick and plastic and attached so tightly I'm afraid of ripping it off because of the noise it might make.

When I step through the revolving door into the antechamber I hear the Sex Room's self-cleaning function go into effect. A loud hiss of water pressure vibrates the floor and the walls. I am now required to shower. The shower in the antechamber turns on automatically. The thing she attached to my leg is a small package wrapped in a shrink-wrap whose color very closely matches my skin. I, therefore, step into the shower and scrub my entire body clean. I am tempted to rip the package off my leg and have a look, but decide it would be best to do it in my quarters, since that is where she implied she wanted me to do it. Perhaps Poppy is testing my common sense with this encounter? It is very difficult to say. I simply have to have faith that this is the case; and if it's not, I have to have faith in Poppy's surveillance system to discern that my intent is not to be clandestine, but compliant.

As the hot mist of the shower rises, this entire experience suddenly feels so unreal I can hardly feel the scalding water touch my body. I step out onto the white tiles and dry myself. I send the towel down the incineration chute. I open the armoire and carefully slip on my underwear and pants and the rest of my clothes. I tie my tie into a firm knot and step out into the lounge. The man who was waiting before me is no longer there. In his place is another and two more beside him. They don't regard me as I walk to the desk.

"If you would, Mr. Louse," the woman says to me as she turns the roster in my direction. She hands me a pen. I sign my name next to the date and time. I hand back the pen. She turns the roster back toward her.

"Good fortune," she says.

"Good fortune," I say.

I walk out into the corridor and go directly to the elevator.

Two men stand on either side of me, wiping a few beads of water from their brow.

RWOOD'S LOG

According to sworn testimony and monitoring of electronic transfers, our missing funds were moved from Nester to Blurd, from Blurd to Olivier, Olivier to Kovax. All security codes malfunctioned or were overwritten. According to depositions witnessed by Wagner, Dougherty, and Kendrick, Kovax admitted to transferring funds to Lumpit, the former Head Controller, who transferred funds to Fordham, the current Head Controller. Fordham was sent a message from Blurd who was acting on orders by the Head Engineer to send the money to Berger. Berger, not knowing what to do with the newest funds, sent them on to Blank. Blank split them and sent them on to Nester and Blurd, who consolidated them and sent them ahead to Lumpit. Lumpit sent them back to Fordham who had sent them to Berger who, at this point corrupted by the Head Engineer, received word to temporarily shelter the funds in a deposit made out to Space Age Technology, Inc.

Space Age Technology, Inc. allegedly sent a receipt for twelve thousand tons of titanium alloy directly to the

Head Engineer, who hid all records and transactions of the receipt, thus making it seem that the receipt no longer existed. Fordham, according to his deposition, assumes that the Head Engineer received it. According to all checks on and efforts to find Space Age Technology, Inc., the company does not exist, though a record of Space Age Technology existing seven years ago does exist and when it did exist it only existed for an exclusive client, namely himself, the Head Engineer who had at the time acquired building materials for Paradise.

This leads me to suspect that Space Age Technology, Inc. has not existed since that point in time (if it ever really existed) and that the funds allocated for Paradise Beyond Paradise are to be found somewhere within the confines of G. More evidence of this emerged when the exact funds allocated to Space Age Technology, Inc. momentarily returned and then disappeared again. The account of Mortimer Blank (to whom the funds were returned), in particular, is impossible to detect since the account's identification code continues to change from one random number to the next. Mortimer Blank has recently left his imprint on the code of Mr. Slodsky. The probability that I will ascertain the whereabouts of the funds without apprehending the Head Engineer are slim to none, at least highly unlikely, but hopefully probable with the aid of an honest Controller.

Without the aid of the Controller, funds cannot be released. Each time I eliminate the Controller, the new Controller is corrupted by the Head Engineer. If the Controller isn't corrupted, funds won't be released and all will be well. But all Controllers have been corrupted. I don't have time to be the Controller. The Controller is altogether consumed with work, especially with the Head Engineer reigning over us. I will order a new Controller immediately.

. THE VIEWIN

When I return to my quarters, I remove my jacket and take a seat on the bed. I can hear the weak buzz of a fly bumping against the window pane. But I don't look. I listen and wait as it pushes away and lethargically circles around the room. I can tell it is a fat little fly and doesn't have much fight in it. It is probably wondering how it is that it actually found its way up the air conditioning shaft to this place, only to find a piece of glass separating it from the outside. The fly buzzes and swoops around my head and lands on my nose. I look at it as it struggles to groom itself. It acts out its instinctual behavior to the very last swipe of its little arms and then slopes down the narrow ridge to fall dead into my lap. I walk the fly to the incinerator in the bathroom, open the door, and watch it disappear into the hot darkness. I go to the toilet and stand before it to relieve myself, wondering how to remove the package from my leg without it looking obvious that I am removing a package from my leg.

I'm unsure if removing the package from my leg in the open is an acceptable thing to do considering how I received it. I don't recall anything within my contract that addresses a situation such as this; which leads me to believe that I should follow my intuition, which should resemble common sense, that is if I am still in my right mind. If my intuition is wrong then I imagine I have failed the test and Poppy or Mr. Sherwood or Dr. Barnum will deal with me in the appropriate manner. There is therefore very little for me to do other than to do what I feel seems most right. And what feels most right at this particular moment is to remove the package in the most subtle way I possibly can to avoid detection of the removal by the cameras. I received the package while it was out of sight; I should remove the package, or at least the contents of the package, so that it remains out of sight.

I walk to the hole between my room and Mr. Crane's room and crouch beside my bed. I find Mr. Crane standing in the middle of the room in his shorts. He is looking up through the skylight as the sound of a plane passes overhead. He stands motionless. I wait for the noise to disappear, thinking of the woman's movements in SR-5, how she crept up my body with such fluidity and how the entire experience was one long, uninterrupted movement. As the drone of the engine drifts away and turns back into the white noise of my quarters, Mr. Crane continues looking through his skylight, gazing up at the muted stars. His large head tilts back onto the fat folds of flesh on his neck as pale moonlight juts down his jaw from his chin.

When I get up, I go to my desk, pull out my chair, and take a seat. I pull my chair under my desk and in an inconspicuous way dislodge the package from my leg by pulling at its corners through my pants. I push it down just below my knee. I then adjust my chair ever so slightly so that I can cross my legs. And then as if to scratch my shin, I reach into my pants leg, slide the package out, and cup it in my hand. I uncross my legs and then roll my chair over to my filing cabinet. I open the cabinet drawer, wedge my hand through the opening in a folder and gently insert the small square of plastic into the file. When this is done, I notice, to my relief, a slit in the section that was taped to my leg. Acting as though I am removing a new document from the file, I remove it from the slit, unfold it, and place it on my desk.

I am nearly sweating when this is through.

I roll my chair away from the filing cabinet and pull the document back to my reading area. To my surprise, it is a copy of my contract; or so it appears to be at first glance. The more I look at it, however, I realize that it isn't at all. Yes, it does contain sections of the contract verbatim; though interspersed between these sections is bold print that looks like the contract, but isn't.

The very first bowdlerized section begins,

> **Mr. Louse—we suggest you do not spend more time with this document than you would normally spend reviewing your contract. As per the basis of our agreement, your presence in the Lounge this evening was an act of engagement on your part. You are heretofore to respect any order we deliver through correspondence or through personal attaché. We now regard you as a sanctioned conspirator and will contact you when it is necessary (continued on p. 2).**

I am stunned at the sight of this. What agreement? I never made an agreement other than the official agreements.

I turn the page and search through the fine print.

> I can only imagine what you think of
> this unorthodox communication, but I
> assure you that the information you just
> read on p. 1 will now be of the greatest
> interest to you. Let me introduce myself,
> Mr. Louse. I am part of a small organiza-
> tion whose purpose is to subvert the best
> interests of G.

Mortimer Blank no doubt! Who else could it be?

> Our organization is officially sanctioned
> by the Executive Controlling Partner,
> though, simultaneously, our members
> remain partially anonymous and our
> directives remain partially unknown to
> the above-mentioned party. The theory
> behind our group is, as Mr. Blackwell has
> written, "If there is no enemy within,
> there is no enemy to fight." Whether it be
> your good fortune or bad, Mr. Louse, you
> have been chosen to take part in an
> action against the above-mentioned
> party, as well as the parties he is in direct
> opposition to, in order to protect his best
> interests, as well as theirs and your own.
> You may pursue one of two options:

1) You willfully submit your services at the request of the organization when a representative approaches you, or 2) You willfully submit yourself to Internal Affairs and plead innocence as they watch you receive the document you are reading. Now with that in mind, Mr. Louse...

I stop reading for a moment and weigh the two alternatives, wondering which would be the best, and wondering how he could keep them from reading what I am currently reading unless this individual is part of Intelligence or Internal Affairs or has similar capabilities as those in Intelligence or Internal Affairs.

they will no doubt determine that you have taken on the role of a sanctioned conspirator; they will deal with you appropriately, as you will see them do to Ms. Berger this evening, as well as to other such traitors and conspirators you have seen corrected in the past. On the other hand, Mr. Louse, if you submit your services, there will be no need for us to call this indiscretion to any one's attention. It will pass without a trace, as opposed to having the incident run off the lips of each and every member of G. as they watch your viewing in the Great Hall.

There is no reason for me to believe that any of this information is incredible. It makes perfect sense. There is nothing I know of Poppy that wouldn't suggest he is capable of such contradictions to simultaneously set up a group opposed to him and his enemies.

But where does this leave me?

Why should I care who wins and who loses and who's allied with whom? All I can see for the time being is my body at the hands of Dr. Barnum should I report this incident to him or Mr. Sherwood or even to Poppy, especially since I would have to speak to Poppy, to utter the words that would give it all away. If I remain silent, and it is true that Mr. Blank will hide this moment in time from Intelligence and Internal Affairs, as long as I am complicit, why shouldn't I remain silent? Then again, what if he can't? What if he can't hide this and it's all a bluff? What then? What will I say to Dr. Barnum when he is interrogating me and there is nothing to say? Then again, what will he ask when he already believes that I have taken part in a plot against him and all else? Won't the questions be the same, as well as his methods?

There is a knock at the door.

I quickly slip the document into the filing cabinet, shut the drawer firmly, and walk across the room. When I open the door, I find Mr. Crane standing before me; the entire domestic staff lumbers down the hall to the off-duty elevator at the end of the wing.

"Will you be going to the viewing, Mr. Louse?" asks Mr. Crane.

"Yes, of course," I say, looking at my watch nervously. "But first I must stop and see the collections official."

"Well, it's on the way," says Mr. Crane as I step into the wing and get swept up by the crowd.

"Yes, yes it is."

"Mr. Louse?!" Mr. Lutherford says, greeting me from behind. "I understand you had a fainting spell."

"Hope you didn't fall into harm's way," says Mr. Heinrik, who is beside Mr. Lutherford.

"Thank you, Mr. Heinrik," I say, although I can feel his sarcasm resonate with every breath and can imagine his eyes meeting Mr. Lutherford's with the secret jokes they have between them. If they only knew what I knew they would truly have secrets between them.

The silver doors of the elevator open.

We step into the silver interior.

We descend toward the twenty-third floor.

"I understand Ms. Berger has been to see Dr. Barnum," Mr. Crane says to Mr. Lutherford.

"She's the first to be corrected in this matter," says Mr. Heinrik.

"It should be interesting to see what he's done to her," says Lutherford.

"I say she gets what she deserves," says another behind us. "She was very devious!"

"Clandestine!"

"I understand the Head Engineer is involved on some level."

"Is that so?"

"It's the newest news."

"It's rare to have someone so high up represented."

"I've always been suspicious of that one, however."

"How so?"

"He's a loner. A recluse."

"Has anyone ever seen him?"

"I once had to deliver a note to him."

"And?"

"He wouldn't open the door."

"You see!"

"He spoke to me over the intercom. He was very rude. Broke every rule. Ignored protocol."

"I believe they will find whatever they expect to find with that one."

"With this Ms. Berger too, no doubt."

"And that Blank."

"Yes, that Blank."

"It is only a matter of time."

"Yes, only a matter of time."

The elevator comes to a halt.

The doors open.

We file out into the staff gaming room.

The room opens up long and wide and is decorated in the greens and reds of the casino downstairs. The ceilings are vaulted, the chandeliers crystal, all the tables rosewood and unblemished felts. A huge mosaic of Union cavalrymen with rifles chasing Indians with spears wraps around the room. In the background and foreground are Indian tribes ascending over mountains and down into plains where they are huddled into encampments. There are pioneers on trails and miners panning for gold; trading posts covered in buffalo pelts and blankets; military forts and rodeo shows; Christian missionaries and evangelist preachers; railroad tracks and chain gangs; cowboy saloons with dancing girls and poker players; oil rigs spouting black velum and creeks littered with rotting cattle; fields of broken skeletons, skulls mounted on sticks, wild horses vanishing onto horizon lines above which are the glowing white hands of God descending from space.

The room is generally crowded, but conversation does not rise above the hush of whispers. The slot machines don't ring, the pit bosses don't bark, the staff members are not allowed to get impassioned when they win or lose. If they do, they are escorted to the outer wings and lose their privileges for a period of time.

As the others continue on to the Great Hall, I am intercepted by Mr. Dulcimer, a tall and skinny cleaning foreman from the fourteenth floor. He always latches onto me ostensibly for the sake of company, but really for the deliberate intention of being persistent. He thinks—because of my position on the thirty-third floor—I always know more than he does. As much as I would love to avoid him, I'm afraid that if I'm uncooperative he'll think he is being shunned and make a complaint.

"Have you heard the latest, Mr. Louse?" Mr. Dulcimer whispers.

"Of Ms. Berger?" I whisper back.

"Yes, of Ms. Berger," says Mr. Dulcimer. "Everyone's talking about it."

"What have you heard, Mr. Dulcimer?"

"Well, I've only been able to pick up bits and pieces thus far, but I've learned that she is new to the Sales Department and was demoted from the ranks of Internal Affairs. I'm not sure why, but for her part in the scandal at hand, no doubt. As you know, they don't demote anyone from Internal Affairs unless a serious offense has been committed. And so you know a very serious offense has been committed, Mr. Louse. You, of course, remember the incident when Mr. Doolittle was excluded for his deviousness?"

"Oh, yes, of course," I say.

"Yes, of course," he says. "And the time Mr. Trillstein from Detentions created his own misfortunes?"

"Yes, I remember, Mr. Dulcimer. I remember very well."

Mr. Dulcimer shakes his head in such a way that a small bit of loose flesh dances about under his chin. "It's all very serious business, Mr. Louse. They are not going to look upon this lightly."

"No, I imagine not, Mr. Dulcimer," I say as I notice Ms. Lonesome sitting at a blackjack table across from me, directly under the belly of a horse saddled with a cavalryman whose bullet is careening toward a young Indian woman with a baby in her arms. Ms. Lonesome and I are facing each other; however, because she's engaged in her cards she doesn't see me.

"Mr. Louse," Mr. Dulcimer continues.

"Yes, I'm sorry, Mr. Dulcimer," I say, turning my attention back to him.

"There is more, Mr. Louse."

"Please," I insist, "go on."

"You're familiar with Mr. Moorcraft, the Head Engineer, I assume?"

"Yes, Mr. Dulcimer, I have heard mention of the Head Engineer."

"Well, Intelligence has begun an extensive search for him. It is really quite thrilling, and by far the most dramatic event known to the Resort Town of G. The Head Engineer is known to be threatening G. with a cache of explosives sizable enough to destroy us all. It's treason, Mr. Louse! Treason!"

"Yes," I say gravely, thinking of my role in this. "That is a new development," I add.

"Intelligence is looking into it."

"And the best of fortune to them," I say.

"Indeed," says Mr. Dulcimer. "They say that Mr. Moorcraft is clever and has the ability to walk invisibly and silently among us. It would be the greatest catch should anyone turn him in. Internal Affairs reports a total and complete absolution for anyone leading to the arrest of the Head Engineer."

"I will keep that in mind, Mr. Dulcimer."

"As you should, Mr. Louse. As we all should."

Mr. Dulcimer stands before me a moment longer; together we look over the activity of the room. I notice Ms. Lonesome make a bet and then glance up to the hands of God. As she looks down, she looks across the room and meets my eye. Her gaze remains fixed on mine and then she looks back down to her cards.

"Well, Mr. Dulcimer, you'll have to excuse me," I say looking at my watch. "I have an appointment with the collections official."

"Please, Mr. Louse, I don't want to keep you."

"Thank you, Mr. Dulcimer."

"Good fortune to you, Mr. Louse."

"Good fortune to you, Mr. Dulcimer," I say turning away from him.

"Oh, Mr. Louse. I almost forgot," Mr. Dulcimer says.

I turn back to him.

"I was given this letter to give to you. For after the viewing."

I cautiously take the envelope from Mr. Dulcimer's hand. "Who is this from?"

"In all honesty I don't know, Mr. Louse. He was in a rush to tend to some duty. He saw you coming and asked me to hand you this."

Mr. Dulcimer smiles candidly and shrugs his shoulders. "In any case, Mr. Louse…" And then he turns away from me looking complete. He sees Mr. Dean, a well-mannered sales representative, enter the room and follows after him.

I stuff the envelope into the inside pocket of my jacket.

Mr. Hamilton, the collections official, is very stern, a thin, gaunt man with thick salt and pepper hair receding above a patrician brow. His complexion and attire make him a well-suited figure for the gaming room: His nose looks like a waterlogged strawberry; he wears a green felt tie that pinches his Adam's apple and turns his cheeks ruddy. He sits behind a window much like that of a bank teller in one of Poppy's old Western films. The window is oval, has vertical metal bars and a slot just large enough for a small pair of hands.

"Good evening, Mr. Hamilton," I say as I approach the counter.

"Good evening, Mr. Louse. I will only be a moment," he says brusquely. He turns away from me and anxiously clicks his tongue as he tabulates my figures.

Two short lines queued up for the cashiers on either side of Mr. Hamilton's station make an elaborate cacophony of whispers.

"She must be connected to him."

"Yes, I know."

"If the threats are what they say they are!"

"Oh, if the threat is what they say it is!"

"Far be it for me to say she set a new precedent, but…"

"This must be the first time."

"What if she claims it wasn't her at all?"

"Denial of her actions will only reap a more stringent reprisal."

"And you can just imagine."

"Oooo, I don't even wish to think."

"It should be quite spectacular."

"He will go to great lengths."

"Especially in light of the circumstances."

"I only wish this line would move faster."

"Shall we?"

"Yes, I think we should."

"We'll…"

"After the…"

"Yes!"

And with that, a good portion of the crowd drops off in the direction of the Great Hall.

"Here we are, Mr. Louse," Mr. Hamilton says, looking away to the others drifting into the corridor at the end of the gaming room. He looks back to me and hands me a receipt with a queer smile on his lips. "Good fortune to you, Mr. Louse," he says appropriately, and shuts his window before I have the chance to thank him.

"With the current interest rates holding at 19 percent…," it reads. It is apparent that my punishment has been levied. I now owe twice as much as I did a week ago but less than two months ago. In short, my debt has been nearly doubled.

I remove a pen from the inside pocket of my jacket and sign the dotted line, indicating that I have updated my files. I remove the borrower's copy, and insert the trustee's copy into Mr. Hamilton's deposit box.

When I turn around I find Ms. Lonesome behind me.

"Good evening, Ms. Lonesome," I say.

"Good evening, Mr. Louse," she says.

"On your way to the Great Hall?" I ask.

"Yes, Mr. Louse."

"Do you mind if I join you?"

"No, not at all."

Ms. Lonesome and I follow the others through the corridor leading to the Great Hall.

"I understand tonight's viewing will be unlike any other," she says.

"Yes, that's what I've heard," I confirm.

Ms. Lonesome occasionally looks at me as we walk. She has put her hair up into a bun since I last saw her. With her hair up, she is poised in such a way that when she talks the tendons in her neck revealed by the open collar of her blouse become attenuated. They flex and stretch into the small triangle of flesh just below the dimple of her trachea.

"I hope they find Mr. Blank and Mr. Moorcraft before any damage is done," Ms. Lonesome says.

"Yes," I say.

"Yes," she says.

She looks at me, expressionless, as if to punctuate her last statement with cold conviction. But she is not convincing. Her features are too soft, her cheeks too round. She almost looks ridiculous acting in such a manner. However, I do understand her compunction to do so. The pulse of red lights from the surveillance cameras spreads across the pale pink pallor of her lips.

We walk through a long, dim hallway at the end of which is a pair of tall double doors. A narrow slit of light runs through them.

It extends outward in a thin beam that meets the toes of our shoes. We follow the thin line over the slick linoleum.

Pictures of Managers and Middle Managers of the Month with broad smiles cover the walls. Upon every new step, two new pairs of eyes stare at us. Camera lights flash off their pupils and the bold, gilded borders of the frames. The corridor is silent. All I can hear is the clomping of our shoes.

When we reach the doors I take hold of the handles, and, as I pull at them, a wave of boisterous gossip momentarily deafens me. The after-hours staff has convened.

"Please, after you!" I shout at Ms. Lonesome.

"You're very kind, Mr. Louse!"

The Great Hall opens up like the inside of an immense diamond. The ceiling rises one hundred feet if not more. Dozens of long, glass banquet tables and benches extend from the entrance to the opposite end of the room. The ceiling and walls are made of glass and steel. Narrow, empty catwalks and rectangular light fixtures appear to hover in midair. The fixtures light the tables and benches stark white and crackle and buzz with annoying fluorescent flickers. Big screen televisions hang from the ceiling by thick shimmering rods. The screens glow cobalt blue and add a hum to the buzz and flicker of the lights.

We pass Venison and the other supply clerks. We pass the table lined with clerical staff. Everyone stands at attention before steaming trays of beef and potatoes, a cup of soup, a slice of bread. We walk to the very center of the room where we take our places among the domestic personnel. I step over the bench and stand at attention between Mr. Lutherford and Mr. Crane. Ms. Lonesome takes a seat directly across from me next to Ms. Morris. As she steps over the bench, a screen running the length of the front wall rapidly descends from a long, narrow box. When it has fully unraveled, the lights of the Great Hall slowly dim and we all sit, all except one: Ms. Berger, the lone sales representative whose transgression has brought about this spectacle. The room becomes still. As all traces of conversation dwindle into coughs and a few stray whispers, a spotlight flashes on Ms. Berger. At the exact same moment, her image is projected onto the large screen. She is a petite woman with short blond hair and full lips. Her cheeks are bright red, her green eyes bloodshot and glassy. Within the column of light, every tiny pore and imperfection in her skin is enhanced; I can even see dust particles floating around her hands and waist.

All heads turn toward the televisions hanging from the ceiling. Ms. Berger's head turns as well.

She, along with everyone else, is ready to watch her correction.

All of a sudden the hundreds of screens throughout the cafeteria turn from blue to black and then display the logo of the Resort Town of G., a skyscraper eclipsing the setting sun. The image lingers for a few moments, filling the Great Hall with a golden glow. As the light shines brightest, the camera's point of view shifts to the back of a limousine, which is parked under an overhang that looks like a luminescent pair of steel wings. The car door opens and we enter the casino, whose staff lavish smiles and upturned thumbs at passersby. A woman hits a jackpot on the slot machine. A man surrounded by toddlers in highchairs piles chips into mounds at a craps table. An usher escorts a couple of bejeweled high rollers through a cheering studio audience. In the distance, a tall, dapper man dressed in top hat and tails walks from behind a red curtain. The camera closes in on him and he announces:

"Welcome to the wonderful world of 'Beyond Temptation,' brought to you by your proud sponsors at the Resort Town of G., where our motto is 'There is safety in numbers.' Tonight we are honored to be presenting Ms. Florence Berger, debtor and sales representative. She will be assisting Dr. Barnum in a presentation on defiance, free will, and personal neglect. Ms. Berger is accused of *conspiracy*."

The studio audience applauds and the man waves his right hand toward the curtain. The curtain opens, presenting Ms. Berger in full color. She is naked, submerged in a glass tank of water. Her feet are shackled to the bottom, her arms to the sides. The water covers her upper lip, which makes it so she must breathe through her nose. When she exhales, the water's surface ripples into the shape of small arrows.

Dr. Barnum smiles a wide, magnanimous smile at the audience. He slowly lifts his arms above his head, gyrating his wrists until his arms are extended upwards in a V. He snaps his fingers and raises his chin.

The audience applauds.

Then Dr. Barnum, as if presenting the farce of all farces, bounds off stage right.

The audience in the video continues applauding. The audience in the Great Hall applauds. The room rumbles with applause. I, given this cue, applaud with the rest.

"A new conceit," says Mr. Crane to Mr. Lutherford.

"Brilliant," Mr. Lutherford responds.

"He is true genius," Ms. Morris beams.

As the applause dies down, the Great Hall continues to murmur in wonder at Dr. Barnum's newest concept.

There is a twenty-four hour clock in the corner of the television screen that shows us the time period over which Ms. Berger's correction took place. As the process begins, we soon learn that Dr. Barnum used a method of time lapse photography to present this to us. After the first hour ticks off, it becomes apparent that for every one of Ms. Berger's hours, a half minute or so passes for us.

A slow and bittersweet sound track of accordion music plays along with the action. Whenever Ms. Berger blinks there is a fluttering of keys and when she begins to slouch, the music swoons. We sit silently, listening. I carefully watch Ms. Berger's muscles, searching for twitches or spasms, any kind of movement. During the first several of our minutes, her hours, she manages to stand erect in the tank. The music remains melancholic and calm. Come her fifth hour, however, she begins to slouch a bit so that her nose inches dangerously close to the water. The music swoons when she does this. And when, in the sixth hour, she begins to squirm, her body undulates a little and leans forward and back until her nose finally touches the surface and slightly goes under. Here, there is a resounding gasp all across the hall as the music jumps across the keyboard and Ms. Berger is zapped with electricity and a garish and magnificent shade of purple explodes in the background. Ms. Berger jumps to an erect position once again. Her eyes open wide in shock. Her nose flares as she pulls in a deep breath.

"Oh my!" Mr. Heinrik nearly cries out as a wide smile forms across his face, followed by a short staccato "Oh-ho-ho-ho."

A laugh track is introduced. And as we did with the applause, those who aren't already laughing, laugh along. I can see that Ms. Berger, as she sits in the Great Hall, is sweating and wringing her hands; she, according to the rules and regulations, must laugh and applaud with us. She does this obediently, but obviously not without great distress.

The viewing continues in this way.

Each time she falls close to the water, each time she comes dangerously close to falling asleep, the harsh crackle of electricity resounds and a new vibrant color flashes behind her. The laugh track sounds off. We laugh. She laughs with us. On it goes this way until the sixteenth hour in Ms. Berger's time. In the sixteenth hour Dr. Barnum walks back out onto the stage. We applaud his presence. He makes a slight bow for us, then taps the glass of the tank to get Ms. Berger's attention.

In his hand is a bunch of grapes. He fastens them to a small grappling hook. The doctor raises his hands to the grapes as they are lifted away. We applaud him once again. He bows and then, once again, exits the stage.

When the grapes reach the mouth of the tank, they are lowered to a height just above Ms. Berger's head, just before her eyes. She tries to ignore them at first, but eventually attempts to push her lips above the water. However, she can't. She struggles to move her arms but can't. Her eyes are fixed on the food and—even if she isn't—she looks desperately hungry. No longer able to control the humiliation and frustration she feels, she begins to cry. Tears stream out her eyes, over her cheeks, and drip into the water as her mouth twists in and out of a tragic mask. She then collects herself momentarily and, spontaneously, makes an irrational movement to break free. She thrashes around like a hooked fish. She wiggles her body, jumps against the restraints holding her feet to the bottom of the tank, falls forward and back to the point that she dips her head into the water. The crackle of electricity resounds, the accordion music builds faster and faster, all the colors that have come before pulsate in the background; and finally, she becomes still again. Her face is haggard, her eyes are swollen, her cheeks drag on her bones.

The curtains swoosh closed.

There is a loud round of applause. We all clap in unison with each other in a celebratory rhythm until Dr. Barnum parts the curtains. We continue clapping as he takes a final bow, steps back, and disappears.

There are applause and whistles; we applaud and whistle, until the lights of the Great Hall burst on.

The televisions fade to black, then blue. The screen in the front recoils into the wall. And poor Ms. Berger sits down beside her colleagues. She sits before her tray, poised with fork and knife in hand. She doesn't move. She doesn't blink.

"A necessary means to an end," Mr. Heinrik says.

"An appropriate measure by all means," Ms. Morris comments.

"Conspiracy and treason bring the doctor much inspiration," says Mr. Crane.

"Revivifying," says Mr. Lutherford with a smile.

"An unfortunate necessity," I say.

"Yes, an unfortunate necessity," Ms. Lonesome agrees.

The others look at us disapprovingly and shake their heads.

We all lift our forks in unison and begin eating. There is more talk around me of Ms. Berger's transgression. The entire room grumbles with it.

"The news is coming close to home these days," Ms. Morris says, changing the subject.

"Yes, very close," Mr. Crane agrees.

"That Mr. Slodsky…," Lutherford conjoins.

"Yes, Slodsky," Heinrik echoes.

"What is the news?" I ask, looking up from my meal, feeling a great need to know.

"He's been connected to Berger."

"He's crossed paths with Blank."

"He's made deliveries to Moorcraft."

"Wandered into Accounting."

"His name was in the vault."

"On the list."

"Face up in the trunk."

"They say he shared secret information…"

"That helped launder money away from Paradise."

"He was promised a personal account."

"Benefits."

"Access."

"They're saying if it weren't for Slodsky, Blank wouldn't have his grip on G."

"He's prevented progress."

"Kept us from Paradise."

"Betrayed the Executive."

"Betrayed us all!"

"From what I understand, all the conspirators were contacted in the Sex Rooms and were given instructions from there," Heinrik boasts.

"That's what they're saying," Ms. Morris continues. "They're saying he went to the Lounge and was given his instructions."

"Coercive measures."

"Very much so."

"But they haven't said who it is who acted as intermediary?"

"No."

"They must know."

"Oh, no doubt. But you know they don't disclose everything at once."

"We should be hearing momentarily then. Don't you think, Mr. Louse?"

"Surely," I say. "Yes, absolutely."

"Yes," Mr. Lutherford agrees. And the others continue their gossip.

My throat suddenly feels tight, my stomach soured. I quickly take my last few bites of meat and potatoes as I think of Mr. Slodsky's fate, of my own. I can no longer listen to this conversation without knowing if my anxiety is not becoming transparent. I swipe my bread across my plate and drink my water.

"Excuse me," I say to Ms. Lonesome.

"Yes, of course," she says, obviously a little startled at my abrupt departure.

I look to the others with as much confidence as I can possibly muster.

"Yes, of course," the rest say.

I step away from the bench and walk down the long corridor back to the tall double doors. I trail behind a small cluster of managerial consultants. We pass Ms. Berger's table. She is still sitting catatonic before her tray. She doesn't flinch when we pass her. She doesn't flinch at the conversation bustling at her own table.

"They say there is nothing to fear," says the managerial consultant walking in front of me.

"Intelligence is currently locating the Head Engineer."

"Intelligence is everywhere."

"They say he is invisible."

"They will detect him."

"With the first false move, he will be caught."

"The reports are very optimistic."

"They only see it as a slight delay."

"A temporary set-back."

"They say these things are bound to happen."

"Normalcy wouldn't be normalcy without them."

"When we plan we must expect such interference."

"It is just this matter of the money," one continues.

"Yes, money."

"Intelligence will ferret that out as well."

"They have found the vault."

"They have found the trunk."

"These shameless actions of Blank can't be hidden for long."

"He may be clever, but he is only one man."

"His alliances will be severed soon enough."

"A poor conclusion."

"No doubt."

"No doubt."

When we reach the end of the hall, we stand in a cluster and wait for the elevator. I remove from my jacket pocket the letter Mr. Dulcimer delivered to me in the staff gaming room, and open it.

Mr. Louse:
When you return to the thirty-third floor, Mr. Blackwell will command you to perform an unpleasant task, one you will not think safe. I write this letter to inform you that you are to act counterintuitively; this duty you are to perform

will afford you and others safe passage to the future. Failure to follow through with this task will lead to the worst possible outcome. If you hesitate, you will be arrested and interrogated in the most unpleasant manner. Please take this warning to heart. You will not have a second chance.

Yours sincerely,

Mortimer Blank

Sanctioned Conspirator

When I reach the signature at the bottom of the letter I promptly fold it up and stuff it back into the envelope, which I promptly stuff back into my pocket. I look to my right and my left to be sure no one was reading over my shoulder, feeling panicked, thinking, why? Knowing there is no answer for me.

The elevator doors open.

I step in and ride up.

AL AFFAIRS VI

"Yes or no, Ms. Berger?"

"No, Dr. Barnum."

"Yes or no, Ms. Berger?"

"Yes, Dr. Barnum."

"Did Kovax or Blurd approach you? Yes or no, Ms. Berger?"

"No, Dr. Barnum."

"Did Nester or Blurd approach you? Yes or no, Ms. Berger?"

"No, Dr. Barnum."

"Did Blurd or Blurd approach you?"

"Yes, Dr. Barnum."

"Did Blurd say he was the one who led you to the funds?"

"No, Dr. Barnum."

"What did I say, Ms. Berger?"

"Yes, Dr. Barnum."

"No no. What did I say?"

"I don't know. I don't remember, Dr. Barnum."

"A little juice, Mr. Bartleby."

"Aaaaa! Aaaaa! Oh…oh god oh god pleeeeeeaaaaaase oh god!"

"Did Blurd say he was the one who led you to the file?"

"Did Blurd say he was the one who led you to the file?"

"Blurd said he was the one who led you to the file."

"Blurd said he was the one who led you to the file."

"Blurd said he put the money in the account."

"Blurd said he put the money in the account."

"Blurd said I put the money in the account."

"Blurd said I put the money in the account."

"Was it you, Ms. Berger, who transferred the funds?"

"No, Dr. Barnum."

"Then who was it?"

"Blurd."

"But Blurd said it was you."

"But Blurd said it was me."

"Bring up the juice, Mr. Bartleby!"

"Aaaaaaaaa!!!!! Aaaaaaaaa!!!!!"

12. LAST WISHES

. LAST WISHE

When I exit the off-duty elevator on the thirty-third floor, Mr. Slodsky is standing before me.

"M-M-M-Mr. Louse," Mr. Slodsky stammers. He is desperate, very desperate. His forehead is sweating and his hands are shaking.

"What is it, Mr. Slodsky?" I ask, stepping past him. His nervousness quickly creeps into my breath, which makes me realize I would be best off if I avoided him.

"M-M-Mr. Blackwell is aw-waiting your arrival. He says to come immediately. I have b-b-b-been dismissed."

"Yes, all right," I say. "Thank you for informing me, Mr. Slodsky."

"Y-y-you're welcome, M-M-Mr. Louse. Do you m-m-mind if I walk with you?"

"No, not at all," I lie, wishing he would leave me.

"It's just that I ha-have s-s-some m-m-more to say to you."

"More to say of what, Mr. Slodsky?"

"M-m-more…M-M-Mr. Louse."

"If you don't mind my asking, Mr. Slodsky, why have you chosen to tell me your news? Why not retire and enjoy your time off?"

"B-b…Because, Mr. Louse…," he says letting out a great long breath.

I look over to him.

He looks at me, and then looks at his hands and then looks at me again as though I should already know the answer to my question. I nod my head as though I am ready to hear what he has to say. Mr. Slodsky rolls his eyes up into the back of his head in search of some serenity but can't seem to find any.

"P-P-Pan Opticon is rep-p-porting…n-n-new news of one of P-P-Poppy's attendants, you s-s-see."

I stop walking.

Mr. Slodsky stops with me.

"Yes, Mr. Slodsky, I've already heard the news," I say coldly.

I look at him with his back to one of the glass cases filled with paper planes. And as I look at the horror on his face, a shock of fear runs up my back.

"Th-they are s-s-saying that I am inv-volved with a group of sanctioned c-c-conspirators."

"I don't know what you are talking of, Mr. Slodsky," I say, feeling the weight of Mortimer Blank's letter pressing upon my chest.

Mr. Slodsky's eyes become panicked. As they are about to roll into the back of his head, I turn away from him and continue walking down the hall.

"Th-they say I'm g-g-g-going to be arrested," he says, trailing after me.

I don't say anything to him. I choose to remain silent for my own self-protection and begin walking faster.

"Th-th-they say that I am p-p-partly responsible for the p-p-predicament w-w-we're in. Th-th-they're saying…m-m-many things,

M-M-Mr. Louse... Please...," he continues. But I can't understand anything he says. All I can hear is the sound of his voice muffling the hum of the air conditioner when I hear him scream, "You see! You see!"

"You see!" he screams again.

I stop walking and turn around to find Mr. Slodsky looking back to Mr. Bender and Mr. Godmeyer, who are turning the corner of the south wing.

"You see!" he screams again, this time directly into a camera.

I turn back around and continue walking, not wanting to hear or see any more.

"They will c-come after you," he says. And then all of a sudden Mr. Slodsky's voice is muffled and I can hear his feet kicking at the linoleum as they drag him away. I don't dare turn my head. I continue walking toward Poppy's chambers, trying not to think of the gurgling sound Mr. Slodsky's voice made as it was being dampened.

I continue down the wing toward Poppy's chambers. As I approach the doors, the cellos of Mozart's "Requiem" vibrate the glass of the museum cases. When I enter, Poppy is sitting up in bed. His tray, prepared for his early morning injection, rests on the western night table.

"Mr. Louse, come to the side of my bed," he says with gravity in his voice. "I need to say something."

"Yes, Poppy. Of course."

I walk across the chambers to the bed, where I notice three syringes filled to their last measure; they are set on top of three puffs of white gauze, his rubber tube is all wound up into a circular maze, three empty vials, top to bottom, snugly rest against the lip of the tray.

"Come, Mr. Louse," he says, patting the mattress. "Sit beside me."

"Yes, sir," I say nervously, wondering what exactly he has in mind.

I cautiously sit down, unable to remove my eyes from the three syringes.

"Closer, Herman."

"Yes, sir."

I inch up the bed so that our faces are nearly touching each other. He raises his left arm, takes hold of my face with his hand, and turns it toward him. I can feel his trembling finger nails curl around the back of my ear. When my eyes meet his, he doesn't blink; all I can think of are his shallow breaths rising in and out of his nose. His pupils tremble with his fingers, back and forth, as though they are becoming detached from whatever holds them in place.

"Will you take pity on me, Mr. Louse?" he asks in a very small, strange voice.

"Of course, Poppy," I say, suddenly feeling great sadness and fear, fearing for myself and all the life beneath us, all for no reason I can understand. But before tears can swell in my own eyes, they swell in the corners of Poppy's eyes. He doesn't make a sound. The water runs down his beard onto the linens. He shuts his eyes and lets go of me. Then, from some place deep within, he points to the tray and says, "All three, Mr. Louse." And with that, Poppy's breathing becomes erratic and his skin begins to bead with sweat. I am unable to talk or move. All I can think of is the letter in my pocket from Mortimer Blank, the thought of what the detonation might feel like, the thought of Karl Arnstedt falling onto the bank of the Thames.

"You needn't be afraid, Mr. Louse," Poppy says.

"I can't, Poppy. I…"

"You will, Mr. Louse."

"I won't!" I say. And with these words enunciated in defiance, I feel an automatic and intense wave of nausea and see an image of myself reflected in a mirror. I'm naked, strapped to a reclining chair. My lips are blue, my clavicle is pronounced, black and blue marks the size of half-dollars cover my body, a fresh laceration runs along the curvature of my left breast. And for some reason, I can feel all the pain I felt whenever this took place.

"You will do this, Mr. Louse. You will do this because there are things you can't yet imagine. You will do this without question and without hesitation if you wish safe passage for yourself and the others."

Poppy's eyes still don't blink. He now talks to me with the energy and magnetism of a young man. I want to say no again, but when I think of saying no, I can see a man gently wrapping black and red wires around his forearm, greeting me with pleasantries like, "I hope you had a nice rest, Mr. Louse," as he delicately drops the thick wires into a deep tub of viscous liquid. And I want to say something to this man in my memory, but I am frozen, literally frozen, clenching down, chattering on a large piece of rubber that is somehow attached to my head.

"Begin with the syringe on your left, Mr. Louse, and work your way to the right," Poppy says as he rolls onto his stomach. "You will understand momentarily. You will understand clearly."

"Yes, Poppy," I say, but wanting to say, "I don't understand." I know, somehow, that I must do what I must do for him, do as Mortimer Blank has instructed me. Do my duty. For I can't do anything else without feeling the pain.

Poppy presses a button on his Zenith Space Commander remote control. The doors to his chambers shut and lock down and the third movement of Mozart's "Requiem" plays forcefully over the chambers' speakers. I remove a pair of rubber gloves and a mask from the western night table. I slip on the gloves. Tie back the mask. I act as I have acted so many times in the past. I hum along to the loud torpor of the music and contemplatively prepare Poppy's leg.

As I wrap the band tightly around his thigh the image of my body reflected in the mirror returns. I can see my penis is pierced with a catheter; a thin green tube runs out of me into a large plastic bag. I can feel the laceration under my left breast, feel the skin folding over into a triangle of fat that jiggles as I shiver. A few frozen rivulets of blood trickle down to my hip. I make a loud whale groan through my sinus cavity, and I continue until I attract the attention of the man with the red and black wires. He removes my mouthpiece, at which point, when I'm finally free to speak, I have no control over my jaw muscles. I grunt a few times deep from within my diaphragm and cough with frustration. "Yes, indeed!" the man says, smiling, promptly replacing the mouthpiece. "Yes, indeed!"

I delicately lift the first syringe, tap away its air bubbles, search for a point of entry and slowly and deeply insert it. I push the plunger halfway. I lift the plunger to mix the blood with the compound. I shoot it hard and can feel it struggle into his vein. The thought of it nearly makes me sick. The thought of pushing death into his veins causes me to turn cold and feel blue. I feel as though I have pushed a knife through his belly and have my fist caught in the viscera. With this pump, I can see the vapor of his breath and the dimming light in his cloudy eyes, which remain open as though shocked by what no human can see or imagine. With the plunger depressed, he now moans with pleasure and breathes without fear. I, on the other hand, begin to shake violently, hardly able to lift the second syringe. I defiantly look up to the surveillance cameras on the ceiling, looking straight into all their lenses simultaneously, showing whomever may be watching that I do not do this alone, that they, if they are watching, are doing this with me. And with that in mind, I plunge the second syringe into Poppy's leg, and push the death deeper into the back of his brain, into the dry chambers of his heart. The liquid spills so easily inside him now, it is as though his body has relaxed, as though his veins, arteries, and corpuscles are conspiring with the needle, commingling with it in an embrace…as if together flesh and metal know it is the last time they will feel each other's presence. And finally, they begin to reject one another with the third injection. My reliable vein, my thin but loyal streak of blue, submerges under the skin and disappears from sight. But too late. I accidentally prod him and push the plunger hard with my anxiety. A bubble forms under the skin and grows to the size of a miniature parachute that slowly but surely deflates. I can't help but stand back from it, thinking that when it withers, I too will moan with a final pleasure that I, like Poppy, will not sense.

EENPLAY NOT

A grainy sepia-toned establishing shot of an oil field. Men, who we first mistake at this distance for prairie dogs, scurry toward a gushing derrick, running and disappearing into the black waves pouring down around them.

> Voice-Over (VO) Hagiography: Herbert Horatio Blackwell was born into humble, but dignified, beginnings. His family resided in the oil town of H., located near the Buffalo Bayou, the marshy tributary linking S. and T. His father was a sheriff and fortune seeker, his mother, a refined debutante from D., etc., etc.

> Hagiography continues.
> Establishing Shot Continues: More and more men, what seems to be an endless supply, run toward the gushing derrick.

> Overdub sound of drills winding in their derricks (blender on slow).

Close-up: Large man wearing cowboy hat and thick mustache steps in front of the camera. Likeness of Herbert Robard Blackwell, father. He smiles, then sneers, then cocks his fist back and knocks the camera to the ground.

Close-up/Point of View (POV) camera: Lens sinks into black mud.

Cut to: Montage of victims suffering from small pox and typhoid fever, signs of yellow fever quarantines, gas light fires, mounds and mounds of bugs and beetles and mosquitoes, etc. ****Lots of beetles. Many beetles.

Begin voice-over of Mr. Blackwell's poor mother and her horrible obsession with the perils of mosquitoes and roaches and flies, etc., etc.

VO: Only on crisp winter days would she take the young Mr. Blackwell out walking, during which time she made him write down all the miserable sights she saw...the sickly children, the scurrying mice...and...

The VO continues on and the images change to stills of the young Mr. Blackwell standing before his family's two story house. He is dressed in a black suit, forcing a smile, standing next to an immense drill bit.

Story of fame and fortune follows, the inestimable wealth, the great genius and tragedy and mysterious illnesses that accompany the great man's great luck.

Live Action—Medium Range/Upper Torso: Mr.

Blackwell lifts his large hand toward the camera and waves the cameraman away. He thrusts his hands into his trousers, turns and walks down the front walk of his home.

Camera Pans Right.

Cut to Handheld: The young Mr. Blackwell walks down the street. His image dissolves into an image of a distant airfield. As we learn of his mother's and his father's deaths, the image of the airfield cuts to the POV of camera following plane in midflight. In the distance is a cityscape covered by cumulus clouds.

VO: He began flying and designing planes, a lifelong dream he acquired while patiently attending to his mother. From her bedroom window he enjoyed watching the biplanes lift into the sky from the distant airfield and fly over the town of H., etc., etc.

The camera's POV shifts to the ground teeming with masses whom we mistake for insects.

The plane descends onto a runway, where a crowd of people are waiting. The plane comes to a halt from crowd's POV. The crowd, en masse, chases after the pilot, Mr. Blackwell. Handheld follows. Some men in the crowd lift him up onto their shoulders and carry him away.

VO: …for great distances and traveled the entire width of the North American continent nonstop, etc.

Cut to documentary footage of Mr. Blackwell riding in a convertible, standing and waving.

VO: People fell out onto the streets to celebrate his arrival. They had ticker-tape parades for him in all the great cities. By the time he traveled back across the country he had become a household name. He was visited by dignitaries from around the world and entertained by all the celebrities and movie moguls of the day.

Mr. Blackwell shakes hands with men in tuxedos, women in gowns, paparazzi cameras flashing in the background.

Cut to documentary footage: Mr. Blackwell walks the back lot of movie studio with a short man wearing a monocle. They approach the ornate cast iron gates of EKG Productions and vigorously shake hands.

VO: In the early years, he directed and starred in *H.A. 13-3*, *Trails of the Golden Horde*, and *Custer's Last Stand*; he later produced scores of others. Simultaneously, he continued designing planes and airports and constructed the ubiquitous Transit Air from the bottom up, etc., etc.

A twin engine Transit Air plane floats above the clouds. A blond stewardess smiles at the camera. A determined pilot pulls the throttle. The plane banks off to the horizon and the rising sun.

VO: EKG Productions grossed more money than any studio in the history of studios. Transit Air was the most successful commercial airliner in the history of airliners…etc., etc.

Roll Title: HERBERT HORATIO BLACKWELL: THE UNTOLD STORY

Establishing Shot: Interior Hotel Suite. Photograph of Mr. Blackwell standing profile to slit in curtain.

VO (voice of Godwin Beeles, Director, Producer, Writer): With all the overwhelming details of such a life, he began to suffer long bouts of insomnia. And the less he slept, the more he thought of his mother and felt his life coming to a close. He had money and fame, but as he reached his midthirties, he could no longer enjoy them. His chronic sleeplessness made him paranoid and depressed. He sequestered himself in hotel suites for months at a time and began hiring detectives to keep track of all his business associates. It was during one of these fierce bouts of depression that he met Felonius Barnum.

A young Dr. Barnum appears on the screen in *Dying With No Tomorrow in Sight*, wearing a mask around his neck and a smock. He is standing over a hospital bed in which the young dying girl stares up to the ceiling. The wife and her blind husband hold each other as they stand in a corner. The woman is weeping.

VO: He had taken a walk out to the club, where Mr. Barnum was soliciting acting work. Felonius Barnum was young, handsome, ambitious, but, in Herbert's eyes, talentless. Upon reviewing his screen tests, his shortcomings were evident. However, his frailties endeared Felonius to Herbert, and this is why Herbert took to him...

Footage of *Dying* continues:

Dr. Barnum turns to the couple. A close-up of his face reveals moistened and haggard eyes. The sound track rises through the VO. It is full of somber horns and strings. "I'm sorry," Dr. Barnum says, almost trembling. "I'm sorry." He throws his hands over his face and barges out of the room. The woman guides the man to the bed by the hand and places his hand on the bed post. Then the woman falls over the dead little girl and gives in to her grief. A close-up of her face reveals strange contortions.

VO: He could read in Barnum that he would remain loyal. He took orders well; Herbert knew he wasn't too proud to be humiliated when push came to shove. The two men became inseparable.

Dying Cont.: Dr. Barnum sobs onto the shoulder of a beautiful nurse.

VO: They dined together, attended parties together, dated the same women.

Montage of women posing for the camera on Blackwell's and Barnum's arms.

VO: And Barnum took care of Mr. Blackwell during his depressions. And Poppy in return cast Barnum in EKG films. But Barnum, as was to be expected, was a wash as an actor.

Dying Cont.: Dr. Barnum delicately pushes the beautiful nurse aside and walks down the dimly lit hall toward a pair of swinging double doors.

VO: Mr. Blackwell, knowing Felonius' limitations as an actor, sent him off to medical school so that he could play out his one successful role on a permanent basis, and in so doing provide Mr. Blackwell with more continuous care. Which he did faithfully for thirty years.

Cut to: Close-up of Helga Zimmerwitz in Lounge 18. She exchanges her seat in the lounge with another woman.

Handheld follows her down the hall.

Cut to: Interior Elevator: Helga Zimmerwitz rides down.

Cut to: Helga Zimmerwitz in her quarters.

VO: When Herbert was young the only insects his mother found beautiful and harmless were butterflies.

Interior Quarters. Helga undresses. She opens her closet and removes a black gown. She lays it on the bed.

Cut to: Helga in the dress.

Cut to: Close-up of Helga's face covered by a veil.

She is now Madame, walking down the western wing to Mr. Blackwell's chambers, passing Dr. Barnum on the way.

Exchange POVs.

Dr. Barnum walks by the camera and disappears.

VO: Herbert orders Madame to bring him butterflies so that he might present them to his mother in the event that there is an afterlife and the world isn't the nightmare he has imagined it to be.

Madame enters Mr. Blackwell's chambers. Herbert's POV. Madame approaches the bed and kneels before him.

Close-up: Madame's face.

VO: A woman has been playing the role of Madame for many years now, since shortly after Herbert crash-landed in the desert outside of L. His knees and lower back were severely traumatized. The pain was so tremendous Barnum put him on triple doses of morphine.

The screen splits in three, showing the three holographic images of Jane Kathryn Betty Blackwell, as displayed in bathrooms.

VO: One night while heavily sedated, Herbert awakened and saw, or was dreaming, that his mother had come to his bedside dressed in mourning and she was carrying a glass case of butterflies. She held it in front of his eyes and told him to dress himself in them when he died so that she would recognize him as he walked through the valley of the shadow of death. She said she would come for him and show him the way away from the hell he was living on earth. From that day on, he began dreaming of the day he would die. He began listening to Mozart's "Requiem" night in and night out, thinking of his own funeral and the ugly things people would have to say about him. And the more he began to think of the ugly things people would say, he began to have this great feeling that he would need to leave something truly great and something absolutely horrific behind to justify their talk.

Cut to: Establishing Shot: Giant mushroom cloud blankets the desert. Soldiers climb out of trenches and run toward it with machine guns in hand. They run into the shadows with their hands over their eyes. The cloud billows higher.

VO: As early as the middle of the century Herbert was already dreaming of space. He began dreaming of rocket ships and space stations and life on other planets. While laid up in bed he began researching and developing plans for rocket ships and satellites. From this came high tech planes and weapons, tanks and artillery, that would be used in all the wars and conflagrations to come.

Herbert stands beside Mr. Sherwood as the two men shake hands. Mr. Sherwood whispers something into Herbert's ear. Herbert whispers something back. The two men smile toward camera flashes popping in the distance.

VO: It was at this time that Herbert joined forces with Ronald Sherwood, an actor from the early EKG days who moved on to arms dealing and who had State Department ties, the very man to whom Herbert entrusted his desires to move into the space industry. And as he talked and dreamed about moving into space, all that he had built on earth was being challenged.

A sweaty black boxer leans over the ropes of a ring and pulls a white woman up by the arms. He cradles her, soaking his sweat into her white taffeta. He pulls her close and kisses her directly on the mouth. She melts in his arms.

VO: People were questioning his business practices and the practices of government that kept him in business. He was questioning all the people coming together and screaming about injustices by men such as himself. He began to hear their voices creeping into his sleep and throughout his waking hours, and all he could hear were their voices buzzing and their millions of cars crawling about the streets.

Train tracks stretch ahead and disappear around a winding mountain pass.

VO: He decided he had had enough of this life and that he would do his important work from a great distance away.

A tunnel approaches. The train tracks disappear.

VO: He sold EKG Productions and then Transit Air. He then chartered a train and traveled across the country once and then twice and then a third time, at which point he stopped at the site that would become the Resort Town of G. He bought the train and lived on it while he built the entire town. When it was complete he was transported from his rail car to his chambers and has never left them since.

The train tracks reappear. Brown hills slope up to a smooth vista. The train slows and stops. Dust rushes past and swoops over nearby brush. A large group of men walk out into the open land. They follow bulldozers. Dump trucks haul away mountains of dirt. An immense crane lifts steel girders to great heights. The Head Engineer stands in the foreground with a roll of blueprints tucked under his arm. A line of concrete mixers stretching out to the horizon drives one by one to masonry men. The Head Engineer confers with the men in hard hats and is followed by Mr. Godmeyer. An immense cylindrical skyscraper with the girth of a lake rises above the desert. It is coral and black, shimmering from the light and the heat. On the building's periphery are rectangular swatches of asphalt and rows of adobe bungalows spiraling out to the edge of the foothills. In the far distance, through a ravine, an oversized billboard in the shape of a pristine golden arrow glistens above an interstate, along which an occasional semi passes or pulls off onto the road leading to the casino.

4. INTRUDERS

When I roll Poppy onto his back, the "Requiem" comes to a close and the doors to his chambers open. The dull sound of a breeze enters from the corridors leading from the bathrooms and from the western wing; it whispers over the discarded newspapers, legal pads, and Kleenex. The wind eventually subsides, but in its place I hear the sound of small, scurrying legs. I turn around to find a large black beetle crawling up and over the floor's rough terrain. I see it, but don't believe I see it. I marvel at it as it stupidly shuffles away from me. It heads in the direction of the linoleum border where a fleet of planes I have yet to encase rest upside down on their wings. I slowly move away from the bed and follow the beetle's big gleaming shell as it drags its thick bottom over the layers of crumpled paper. It scurries until it reaches one of the planes, under which it pushes its way into hiding.

I crouch down to lift the plane when I notice, written on the wings, an inscription: "Take me when I fly out into the valley this morning and forgive me for my sins. I regret..." The words trail inside a neatly creased fold that forms the plane's fuselage.

I look over to Poppy, whose eyes are open but whose mind is so obviously somewhere deep within himself. Under the streaks of red light emanating from the surveillance cameras his body looks as though it is hovering over the bed. In fact, everything in the room feels like it has been elevated above me. Even the inanimate legs of the nightstands and the dark bed frame appear to stand fifteen feet high. I have an uncanny sensation of each object continually rising higher with every one of Poppy's shallow breaths, and that this beetle and I are the only things fixed to the floor.

When I finally pick up the plane, the beetle doesn't move; it remains still, its feelers quivering. I can't help wonder what one thinks when faced with his own inevitable destruction. How does one prepare for premature conclusions? Just as I think this, the beetle dashes off in the direction of another plane. Almost instinctively, as a matter of course, a consequence of reflex, I stand up, lift my shoe, and in one swift motion crush the bug under my heel. I can hear the large shell crack and feel the soft insides spread over the surface of the slick linoleum. When I lift my leg, I can feel the beetle's sticky remains cling to me.

I delicately place Poppy's plane away from the mess and remove Mortimer Blank's letter from the inside pocket of my jacket. Using the envelope, I scrape what's left of the beetle from the floor and my shoe and walk down the corridor to Bathroom Number Three. I pass Jane's shadowed face and go directly to the incinerator at the back of the supply closet. I throw the crushed beetle and Mr. Blank's letter down into the dark heat, and with it, my mask and latex gloves.

Once I secure the incinerator door, I walk back into the bathroom. As I reach the threshold leading to the corridor, I hear, coming from Poppy's quarters, a door slam shut. I don't move. My heart momentarily stops beating. All sound seems to filter somewhere else. There is only silence, and more silence, and then another door slams shut and another door opens. My heart now begins to pound. I continue walking into and down the corridor. When I enter Poppy's room, I encounter a large, robust man entering from Corridor Number One. He is shrouded by a warm, lavender light that outlines a thick head and shoulders. He is tall and paunchy in the chest and the stomach. When his face becomes lit I can see his nose, which is thin, and his jaw, which is slightly hidden by several rolls of flesh.

"How do you do?" he asks from across the room.

"Can I help you?" I ask.

"No," he says as he walks over to Poppy's bed. "You've already helped a good deal."

Because of the way he authoritatively disregards me, I don't feel as though I should question what he is doing, but I must make my motive appear clear.

"Do you have a pass?" I ask.

"No," he says, shaking his head. His hair is sandy brown. Some of it falls boyishly into his eyes as he kneels next to Poppy's bed and begins rummaging through a stack of legal pads piled on the floor. He removes one from the bottom of the pile.

"A name? How about a name?" I ask.

"No name. No pass," he says as he flips through the pad and removes a sheet. He folds it up and places it in the pocket of his jacket.

"I'm afraid I can't accept this," I say. "I require a pass and some form of identification."

"Yes, I know. But this time, you'll ignore protocol, Mr. Louse."

"I'm afraid I can't do that, sir."

"Do you know who I am, Herman?"

"I'm not sure," I say, wondering if it isn't Mortimer Blank, if for no other reason than that he knows who I am and I don't know him. But I don't want to say this name. All I can wonder is if Mr. Sherwood and the rest of Intelligence see what he is doing, if Mr. Sherwood has seen what I have done. The red streaks of the camera surveillance lights continue to pulse. If they are watching, if they have been watching, what would they expect me to do? If they aren't watching why doesn't he tell me what he wants of me? But they can't be watching, because if they were watching I would expect they would have sent someone to take care of him, to take care of me. Unless they are watching and they don't dare touch him.

"He's very clammy," the man says as he takes his hand off Poppy's head.

"I'm afraid I can't allow this," I insist, feeling the need to protect Poppy. He wouldn't approve of anyone touching him without gloves.

"It's all right, Mr. Louse," he says, now taking hold of Poppy's wrist and feeling for his pulse. "He'll never know."

"Please, sir," I say. "If you don't show me your pass I will be forced to call Security."

"Bear with me just a moment longer," he says, concentrating on his watch.

"I really must insist," I say nervously.

He lets go of Poppy's arm, gently places it on the bed, and walks over to me.

"Don't worry yourself, Mr. Louse," the man says abruptly. "Come. Come have a closer look." He grabs me by the hand. "Come and feel him. Feel what he is."

As a reflex, I struggle with him a little. But he is much stronger than I. He pulls me by the arm over to Poppy's bedside and places my hand on his head.

"There, Mr. Louse," he whispers in my ear. "Feel what he is."

I don't say anything. I don't understand what I am supposed to feel. I don't understand why Poppy, with all his aspirations for the future, would decide this for himself. I allow my body to go limp in this man's hands and feel, with my bare palm, the coldness of Poppy's damp skin.

"That's all," the man says. "That's all he is." His grip loosens and his fat lips stretch across his face into a half smile. "When I leave," he says, "do what is most appropriate, Mr. Louse. Is that clear?"

Again I don't say anything.

"I will be in touch soon enough."

With that, he briskly walks away, out of Poppy's chambers, into the western wing. I follow him to the door and watch him pass the kitchen and disappear out of the secured zone. I then go to Poppy's intercom with the direct line to Mr. Sherwood, feeling relieved that I am able to act as I should and not feel conflicted by having to choose one side over the other. All the sounds of Poppy's chambers begin to silence as I think of what I am going to tell Mr. Sherwood. Do I tell him that I suspect this man to be Mr. Blank? Does he already know that Blank has made contact with me and I didn't report it? If he knows this why hasn't he acted? If he knows it and he hasn't acted, does he expect me to tell him?

When I reach for the intercom, I try not to hesitate before I press the button.

"Sherwood, here."

"Mr. Sherwood, I'm sorry to disturb you. This is Herman Q. Louse. A man I have never seen before just visited Poppy's chambers. He didn't have a pass, nor was he willing to reveal his identity."

"Very good, Mr. Louse."

"Shall I file a report?"

"That won't be necessary."

"Shall I take any measure whatsoever, sir?"

"Please report to my office immediately."

"Yes, sir."

I release the button of the intercom and can feel myself trembling inside. I step out into the western wing and let out a small laugh through my nose that sounds like weeping.

15. THE HEAD OF INTELLIGENCE

HEAD OF INTE

The thirty-second floor is comprised of small, self-contained glass offices with glass tables, on top of which are monitors and computers. Men and women sit at the small tables and observe all of G.'s activity. There are hundreds of such offices laid out on a square grid. The men and women wear blinders so that nothing in their peripheral vision will distract them from their work. I have never had a conversation with members of Intelligence and Internal Affairs, other than Mr. Bender. They are, for all intents and purposes, sworn to silence. They can talk among themselves, but with no one from outside their department.

When I step out of the elevator, I notice, inside the glass cubicle beside me, an observer watching a small image of me on a monitor. She doesn't turn to look at me; she begins typing at a furious speed.

Before me, a series of colored lines branch out to various departments: Collections, Corrections, Cancellations, Codes, Inspections and Investigations, and Detentions. I follow a red line to Mr. Sherwood's office—Intelligence. It is a straight line to the opposite end of the building. I pass dozens of glass walls, observing the observers do their jobs. When I reach the very end, I approach a waiting room where a dark-haired woman with alabaster skin rigidly sits upright in her seat; her hands fold over each other and rest on a green blotter. The blotter covers a rosewood desk that sits off to the left of a padded leather door. The woman looks directly at my waist-line and doesn't make any effort to look up.

"Herman Q. Louse to see Mr. Sherwood," I say, trying to capture her attention, trying not to show my feelings, which I'm finding more and more difficult as time passes.

She doesn't respond.

Not knowing what to do, I wait.

The woman occasionally blinks her eyes. She exchanges one hand for the other on her blotter.

After several uncomfortable moments, the leather door opens and Mr. Bender, back-lit by a very bright light, steps out into the waiting room.

"If you'll follow me, Mr. Louse," he says, turning on his heel back into Mr. Sherwood's office.

I follow the crooked shadow of his figure through the door and find that the bright light comes from somewhere outside. The window's scrim is not down. When I look out, I can see the rim of a spotlight hovering atop a nearby rock formation. If I look askance, away from the brightness, I can see out onto a vast stretch of desert littered with dark brush whose cone-shaped shadows point down into a valley from the top of a long sloping hill. Beyond the hill, plumes of yellow dust rise into the atmosphere almost as high as the thirty-second floor. I can also see trucks crawling along a straight and narrow road; their metal reflects like distant stars. The trucks drive down into the valley, to a housing project. The roofs of the houses connect to each other and extend out to a tall wall, which lies at the base of the hill.

Mr. Bender walks through a side door, which he closes behind him. Just then, I notice Mr. Godmeyer standing in the corner. As I am about to step forward to look out the window, he presses a button that lowers the scrim.

As the screen descends, the room turns gray. When my eyes adjust to the new light, I can see before me a large rosewood desk six times the size of the secretary's. A letter-size folder rests on top of a large green blotter. Mr. Godmeyer opens the folder as Mr. Sherwood and Mr. Bender enter through the side door.

Mr. Sherwood approaches me, takes hold of my hand with a thick palm, and pumps several times.

"Mr. Louse, do come in," he says pointing me to a chair in front of his desk. "It's nice to see you in the flesh. Mr. Bender has told me nothing but wonderful things." He smiles and lets go of me. He walks behind his desk and sits in a large leather chair. He leans back, creaking into comfort. Mr. Bender stands behind Mr. Sherwood's chair, just off to the side. Mr. Godmeyer returns to his corner.

I sit in the chair Mr. Sherwood has designated for me and can't help but be suspicious of the positive tone of his greeting. I am also a little put off by Mr. Sherwood's size. He is almost the size of Mr. Godmeyer. He is barrel-chested and has a bald dome head. The oversized cuffs of his jacket and pants sway like bells over his thick wrists and ankles. His voice is throaty and contains the sound of him shifting his weight. He has very acute eyes, dark and piercing, but hidden behind full cheeks. His skin is freckled. His manner is stately.

I cautiously look over to Mr. Godmeyer and try to imagine what wonderful things Mr. Bender imparted to Mr. Sherwood for him to be treating me so kindly. Don't they know what I've done? Don't they know what I have been doing?

"So, Mr. Louse," Mr. Sherwood says, "you must be wondering why I've brought you in tonight?"

"The intruder," I say plainly.

"Oh, yes, right," he says. He looks to Mr. Bender who looks to Mr. Godmeyer. "We'll get to that shortly, Mr. Louse."

"Thank you, sir," I say, relieved that we are moving on to something else.

"No need to thank me, Mr. Louse," he says cordially. Mr. Sherwood begins playing with the edge of the folder as he looks me up and down a little more carefully. His face suggests that he neither approves nor disapproves of what's before him. I try to sit still and not move and allow him to study me.

"Tell me, Mr. Louse," Mr. Sherwood says. He looks down to the folder and flips a few pages. "When Mr. Slodsky approached you earlier—just before his arrest—what exactly did he impart to you?"

The skin under my left eye involuntarily twitches as I consider his question.

"He informed me that he had been relieved of his position and that I should attend to Mr. Blackwell," I say in as steady a voice as I can muster.

"Do you recall him saying anything else?"

"He informed me that he had become one of the accused."

"But you already knew this."

"Yes," I say.

Mr. Sherwood turns a page of the folder. I am not sure where this is leading, but I can feel my palms sweating and can hear a slight quaver in my voice as I speak. Mr. Sherwood removes a pen from the inside pocket of his jacket and scribbles a few things on a piece of paper.

"Did you receive any written correspondence from Mr. Slodsky earlier on?"

"Yes, sir. I received a memo from Mr. Blackwell through Mr. Slodsky."

"From Mr. Blackwell?"

"Yes, through Mr. Slodsky."

Mr. Sherwood scribbles some more.

"Would you mind revealing the contents of that memo to us, Mr. Louse."

There is a soft knock on the door. Mr. Bender steps around the desk, passes me, and opens it. Three men of approximately the same medium height and weight enter and stand behind me. Mr. Bender returns to his position beside Mr. Sherwood.

"Mr. Louse, the contents of the memo," Mr. Sherwood repeats.

"Yes, excuse me, sir. In order to curtail my more primitive predilections, Mr. Blackwell instructed me to visit Lounge Eighteen SR-Five."

"I see," says Mr. Sherwood. "Was there a reason for this?" He flips back through several pages of the file, somewhere in the middle.

"Yes, sir," I admit. "For falling asleep on the job and..." I look over my shoulder to see the profile of one of the men behind me.

"Yes, Mr. Louse?"

"For falling asleep on the job and displaying an act of free will."

"I see," says Mr. Sherwood. He scribbles a few more things into the folder and looks up at me as though he plans to continue writing. "You went to Lounge Eighteen SR-Five?"

"Yes, sir."

"And you returned to your quarters around…"

"I don't recall exactly," I say, feeling nervous, knowing that he knows of the contract. "It was just after the end of the late-night shift."

"At which time…"

"At which time I looked in on Mr. Crane."

"Yes, and…"

"And reviewed my contract," I lie, expecting to feel pain from my lie as I did when I defied Poppy's orders, but I don't. Perhaps because it resembles a little of the truth?

Mr. Sherwood stops writing and slowly looks up from the folder. He looks me over again, then looks up to Mr. Bender. I look back over my shoulder at the three men and then look to Mr. Godmeyer. I suddenly have a vision of myself submerged in Dr. Barnum's tank, craning my neck at a bunch of grapes and feeling the surge of electricity course through my body.

"You reviewed your contract?" Mr. Sherwood reiterates.

"Yes, sir."

"And then what?" he asks without any hesitation, apparently without the slightest suspicion that I'm lying, that he has knowledge of the contents of the bowdlerized contract.

"And then Mr. Crane knocked on my door and I joined the others on their way to the viewing."

"I see," Mr. Sherwood says as he flips through several more pages of the file. He licks his thumb and flips some more. And then flips some more. "I see you had a brief conversation with Mr. Dulcimer?"

"Yes, sir."

"Did you know that he is now one of the accused, Mr. Louse?"

"No, sir. That is new news to me, sir," I stammer.

"What was the nature of your conversation?"

"We talked about the accused. Ms. Berger. Mr. Moorcraft."

"He handed you an envelope?"

"He claimed that someone he didn't know handed him an envelope to hand to me."

"The contents of which were…?"

"Regarding orders."

"Orders."

"Yes, orders."

"From Mortimer Blank?" he asks without accusation, only for the purpose of verification. He raises his brows into two arches.

"Yes, from Mortimer Blank," I say, knowing that I can't say anything otherwise at this point, knowing that I have now been discovered and it is futile to hide anything.

"To the best of your knowledge, Mortimer Blank signed the letter?"

"Yes, sir."

"And what did it say exactly?"

"It said to act counterintuitively when I entered Poppy's presence."

"For what purpose?"

"For an unspecified purpose, sir. It simply said that this is what I should do. Or there would be unpleasant circumstances."

"Have there been any unpleasant circumstances?"

"No, sir. I did what I was told."

"You followed orders."

"To the best of my ability, sir."

"And you've followed them well, Mr. Louse," Mr. Sherwood states emphatically. He shuts my file and then smiles. "You have followed them very well. We just wanted to be sure our surveillance checked out all right. I hope you understand, Herman."

"Yes, sir," I say, not entirely sure of what they know and don't know. Under the circumstances, they appear to be as happy as can be.

"In any case, Mr. Louse," he says lifting his hand to the three men behind me, "I would like you to meet Mr. Wagner."

The man in the middle bends forward a little. "Pleased to meet you," he says.

"Likewise," I say.

"And his two associates, Mr. Kendrick and Mr. Dougherty," Mr. Sherwood continues.

"Pleased to meet you," I say.

"Likewise," the two men say.

"From Legal Affairs," Mr. Sherwood adds as he begins playing with the corners of the folder again. "Now, Mr. Louse," he continues, "the fact of the matter is that we have some very good news for you," he says, smiling, which makes me turn my head to Mr. Bender, who is trying to cast a smile in my direction. And as Mr. Sherwood sees me looking to Mr. Bender, he too looks to Mr. Bender. "Would you like to tell him, Bender?" he says.

"Your number has come up, Mr. Louse," Mr. Bender says.

"That's right, Herman. Your number has come up," Mr. Sherwood confirms.

"My number?"

"Yes, your number came up on the computer tonight," Mr. Sherwood says.

"You beat great odds," Mr. Bender says.

"You're a very lucky man, Mr. Louse," Mr. Sherwood says and pauses, leaving me enough room to contemplate the phrase, *Your number's come up.* "You were chosen from our list of future trustees to fill the newest trustee position," Mr. Sherwood continues.

"Congratulations, Mr. Louse," Mr. Bender says.

"Yes, congratulations," Mr. Sherwood says.

I look at them, dumbfounded, wondering how, in the face of such a tense time, they could be concerned with what must be a trivial matter to them. "Thank you, sirs. I don't know what to say."

"There really is nothing to say, Herman. Consider yourself a fortunate soul."

"I do, sir. I most definitely do," I say, not knowing why I should feel this way, knowing what I know.

"As you should," Mr. Sherwood says. "Let me tell you what's going to happen, Herman. Tomorrow, you will become eligible for the Executive Lottery and your debt is going to be fixed at 16.8 percent annual interest. Considering that the current interest rates are holding steadily at 19 percent and haven't dropped below 17 percent in the past decade, I can safely say that your life is taking a turn for the better."

"What's more, Mr. Louse," Mr. Bender interrupts, "from now on, your time will be measured in relationship to your debt. Depending on the priority of a task, for instance, a certain amount of money will be leveraged against the amount owed. In other words, the more self-sacrifice and the greater the risk you are willing to take on behalf of the organization, the more likely you are to absolve yourself from debt."

"You are one of the organization now, Herman," Mr. Sherwood continues. "A trustee in relation to a future trustee is miles apart. Isn't that so, Mr. Bender?"

"To be a trustee is to be a forward thinker, Mr. Louse."

"Trustees think forward, Herman."

"Just think, Mr. Louse, the possibilities within a trusteeship are enormous."

"You may one day find yourself to be in a position you never believed in a lifetime you could have ever earned."

"If the odds are in your favor…"

"Oh, if the odds are in your favor, Mr. Louse, there is no telling what might be."

"Think forward, Mr. Louse, and there will be good fortune."

"When it comes time to lay the past to rest, let it lay, and we will move onward."

"Together."

"All right, Herman?"

"All right?"

The two men become silent, and as they do there is another explosion outside. This one is bigger than any other I have ever heard. Mr. Sherwood and Mr. Bender flinch a little, but act as though they are undisturbed.

Mr. Sherwood smiles at me.

Mr. Bender smiles at me.

"Yes, sirs," I say after a moment of trying to decipher what has just been said.

"Mr. Wagner," Mr. Sherwood says.

Mr. Wagner steps forward and places a briefcase on top of Mr. Sherwood's desk while Mr. Kendrick and Mr. Dougherty flank my right and left sides. Mr. Wagner opens the briefcase and removes a three-inch-thick packet of paper.

"Mr. Louse," Mr. Wagner says, holding up the packet. "Just to reiterate, I am Mr. Wagner from legal affairs. These are my two associates, Mr. Kendrick and Mr. Dougherty."

"I understand," I say as I marvel at the size of the packet in Mr. Wagner's hand.

"The document placed before you," Mr. Wagner continues, "is your new contract for your new position as trustee. Mr. Sherwood and Mr. Bender have already explained the contents of the document before you, and I can corroborate that what's been said has been sufficient, concise, and thorough. As you already know, Mr. Louse, I am here to represent you as your advocate, to assure you that this form is sound and proper. And I am here to say this form is sound and proper. Mr. Kendrick and Mr. Dougherty are here to act as your witnesses. With that said, Mr. Louse, please sign the form at the indicated Xs and we will be on our way."

Mr. Wagner hands me a pen and opens the document to the middle. I sign the form at the indicated Xs. He flips to the back. I sign near some more Xs.

"Very good, Mr. Louse," Mr. Wagner says, turning the paper to Mr. Kendrick. "Mr. Kendrick."

Mr. Kendrick signs the form and turns the paper to Mr. Dougherty.

"Mr. Dougherty," Mr. Kendrick says.

"Mr. Kendrick," Mr. Dougherty says as he takes the pen.

Mr. Dougherty signs.

"Thank you for your time and patience, Mr. Louse," Mr. Wagner says.

And the three men depart Mr. Sherwood's office.

"All right, then, Mr. Louse?" Mr. Sherwood says, his arms out-stretched.

"Yes, sir," I say. "I am very pleased."

"As I said, Mr. Louse," Mr. Sherwood says, "it is well-deserved. You're doing a fine job."

"Thank you, sir. I really do appreciate it." Without even want-ing to appreciate this gesture, I, for some odd reason, feel myself appreciating it.

"Good. We will be sending a copy of the documents to your quarters for your files."

"Is that all, sir?"

"Yes," he says conclusively.

With that, Mr. Sherwood stands up from his chair.

With that, I stand up from mine.

"And about this intruder, Mr. Louse?" Mr. Sherwood says as he steps before me. He takes my hand again. "Better off to leave well enough alone. Think of it as taken care of," he continues, pumping my hand several times, not letting go. "Trustees think forward, Mr. Louse. Think forward and all will turn out well."

"Yes, Mr. Sherwood. Of course," I say.

Mr. Sherwood lets go of my hand and looks over to Mr. Ben-der who looks over to Mr. Godmeyer, who nods his head.

"Thank you for your time, Herman," Mr. Sherwood says, his cheeks pinching at his eyes. "You may go now."

"Thank you again, gentlemen," I say as I look at each of them in the face. I then turn to leave.

16. THE TRUSTEE

.THE TRUSTE

The silver doors of the elevator open and I step into the empty silver interior.

I press thirty-three and ride up.

My mind is riddled with thoughts of why they would grant me this trusteeship now of all times. Especially when my job performance has declined so drastically. When I have done as much as any of the accused. I can't help but wonder what would have happened tonight if I could have just gone to bed. Perhaps I would have slept. Perhaps I would have slept through the night and not known of anyone's demands on me. Maybe I wouldn't have known the things that I have seen and I could continue to go to my quarters, to chase flies, to go to the gaming room, to play roulette, without the burdens of knowledge, of the responsibility of knowing, that has been thrown upon me this evening. I don't wish to take on more than I already have. Why should I care to be stuck in the middle of anyone's best interests; especially when my best interests are undoubtedly to stay uninvolved? I should be left in peace, allowed the liberty to appreciate the few pleasures I have. I don't wish to be like Karl Arnstedt or the Ruteledge brothers and sacrifice myself in the name of someone else's best interests. If this means that I will continue to suffer through the daily regimen of my life as I know it, so be it. I will suffer. I will suffer for whomever wishes it, practice quality of life, adapt to new rules and regulations as they arise. I will suffer for the consequences of my actions. I will suffer and not complain. What else can a man in my position be expected to do?

The elevator doors open.

I walk the southern wing, back toward Poppy's chambers.

"Ah, there you are, Mr. Louse!" Mr. Lutherford cries from the kitchen door as I turn the corner of the western wing. When I step up to him I can see Mr. Lutherford, Mr. Heinrik, Mr. Crane, Ms. Morris, and several others inside the kitchen, standing around drinking grape NeHi and wearing green and red party hats. They are standing in a semicircle facing the doorway. They begin to sing:

For he's a jolly good fellow / For he's a jolly good fellow / For he's a jolly good fellow! / So say all of us! / So say all of us / So say all of us / For he's a jolly good fellow / For he's a jolly good fellow / For he's a jolly good fel–low! / So say all of us!

I don't say anything to them. I am stunned. I just stare, dumbfounded.

"I told you he wouldn't be of good spirits," whispers Ms. Morris to Mr. Crane, who bobs his head.

"Thank you," I utter, not exactly knowing what I'm thanking them for.

"Is that how a winner should hold himself?" asks Mr. Heinrik.

"I'm sorry. I don't understand," I say, looking around the room, wondering if they have learned of my trusteeship. Everyone looks at each other, slack-jawed, then looks at me, then looks at each other again.

"He doesn't know."

"Maybe it wasn't him."

"Maybe he was indisposed."

"You're a winner," Mr. Heinrik says approaching me. "You came away with the exact numbers in the Keno selection. You've had a great stroke of fortune," he continues, then lowers his voice so no one else can hear. Mr. Heinrik grips my arm tightly and smiles at me angrily. I hardly feel him pinching my flesh. "That's why we're having the party," he says, "The winner of Keno, as if I need to remind you, is allowed a party within their division."

"I'm sorry, Mr. Heinrik. I wasn't playing Keno this evening."

"Well then, someone was playing it for you, weren't they? For you won, Mr. Louse," he continues in his hushed voice. Everyone is looking at us as they silently and dumbly sip on their grape NeHi, as though they are waiting for me to make up my mind.

"Don't spoil it for everyone else, Mr. Louse," Mr. Heinrik concludes as he harshly grits his teeth. Some spittle softly brushes my chin as he lets go of me and turns back to everyone. "What a great stroke of fortune!" he bellows as Mr. Lutherford approaches me and snaps a pointy red cap on my head and as Mr. Crane delicately slips a NeHi into my hand.

I try to muster a smile. I bare my teeth for all to see, and upon seeing this they break back into song.

For he's a jolly good fellow / For he's a jolly good fellow / For he's a jolly good fellow! / So say all of us! / So say all of us / So say all of us / For he's a jolly good fellow / For he's a jolly good fellow / For he's a jolly good fel–low! / So say all of us!

We all lift our NeHis and drink to me.

"That's not so bad now, is it, Mr. Louse?" Mr. Heinrik says.

"Thank you, Mr. Heinrik. It's a wonderful gesture," I say, now being taken away by the need to display a moment of good will.

"You're very welcome," Mr. Heinrik says. "You're one lucky man, Mr. Louse."

"Yes, most definitely," Ms. Morris asserts. "Fortune is smiling on you."

"Thank you, Ms. Morris, and to you all."

"Just think, Mr. Louse," Mr. Lutherford continues, "here you stand with a bottle of grape in your hand while history unfolds around us."

"Yes," Ms. Morris seconds, shaking her head and ticking her tongue against the roof of her mouth. "Today will be a momentous day."

"I don't understand," I say.

"They say the list is complete," Mr. Crane informs me.

"The accountants will be brought to justice as soon as the time is right," Mr. Lutherford follows. "Ms. Berger was just the beginning of it all."

"And now," Mr. Heinrik boasts, with eyes wide, looking as though he has a new piece of information to contribute. He pauses. Everyone looks toward him. "They are positive it goes as high up as the Executive!"

"Really? I hadn't heard that," says Mr. Crane. "Well I knew that he was implicated but I had no idea that they had evidence on him."

"It's been said, Mr. Crane," Mr. Heinrik boasts. "From an acquaintance of an acquaintance of an acquaintance, you know, a Pan Opticon source."

They all shake their heads knowingly.

"We all know what this means then," Mr. Lutherford continues.

"The trustees will be clamoring," Ms. Morris says disappointedly. "I don't know if I will be able to stand them."

"You see, Mr. Louse, a truly historic moment."

"What is it that's been said exactly, Mr. Heinrik?" I ask, almost stuttering, but very earnestly, wondering if it is I who helped make this true. "Are you absolutely sure of what you heard?"

"Am I absolutely sure, Mr. Louse? Is that what you're asking me?" Mr. Heinrik asks, looking at me incredulously, defensively, as though I have just challenged him to a fight.

"Are you absolutely sure?" I repeat earnestly. "What they say about Mr. Blackwell?"

"Yes, I'm sure," he says sharply. He adjusts his cone-shaped hat so that it fits on the very crown of his head. "I wouldn't say it otherwise."

"What exactly did you hear, Mr. Heinrik?"

"I told you what I heard, Mr. Louse. The Executive Controlling Partner has been implicated with the rest, from various sources who have implicated him."

"I see. But you can't be more specific?" I ask. "Have they said how such a thing has come about?"

"I find this very irregular, Mr. Louse," Mr. Heinrik says.

"Yes," Mr. Lutherford seconds. "Your line of questioning is out of line, Mr. Louse. You should watch yourself."

"*Repetition*, according to memo thirty-four sixty-seven," Ms. Morris cites, "*is perfectly reasonable; however repetition may only progress to an affirmation based on rumored facts, but never back to rumored facts already stated since reiteration implies doubt which suggests that the realm of circumspection provided lacks truth.*"

"Yes, Ms. Morris, I understand," I say apologetically. "Please excuse me for my impertinence."

"You had to do it, didn't you, Mr. Louse?" Mr. Heinrik says.

"You couldn't consider us for the moment, could you?" Mr. Lutherford chastises.

"It's no fun anymore," Ms. Morris says, taking off her hat.

"Yes, it's been ruined," Mr. Crane agrees.

As Ms. Morris takes off her hat, everyone does the same.

"I'm sorry," I repeat, slowly dragging the hat off my head. "I'm sorry. Really. Please…I don't know what…"

I bow my head in shame.

"It's all right, Mr. Louse," Mr. Crane assures me.

I look up into Mr. Crane's round face.

"I…," I say, feeling a swoon of emotion take hold of my throat and my stomach, and then realize it is a wave of nausea more powerful than I have ever felt before. I grip myself by the neck and then cover my eyes with my palms, able to feel the round inadequacy of my pupils. I roll them back into my head in search of some serenity. I roll them back until I can feel the veins and arteries straining not to snap.

"It's all right, Mr. Louse," Mr. Crane repeats. "Another time."

After a moment, the wave of nausea passes and I see, one by one, the Domestics line up to dispose of their hats and NeHi in the incinerator next to the wash basin. Ms. Morris walks off to "Cleaning Supplies." Mr. Heinrik and Mr. Lutherford return to "Sterilization." Mr. Crane shlumps off to "Maintenance." And the rest disperse to their respective duties. I stand where I am, unable to move, wondering exactly where I am, trying to see more clearly what I have seen in my mind earlier. This nausea…

"Hello, Mr. Louse."

I turn around.

Ms. Lonesome stands in the doorway leading to the back room of the kitchen.

"Hello, Ms. Lonesome."

Ms. Lonesome looks well rested. There is not a line or a crease in her face or her clothing. Her eyes are lucid and attentive. Her hair is down, brushing against her shoulder as she steps toward me. The sight of her constructs a brief moment of clarity.

"Mr. Louse," she says, "I've been instructed to escort you to Mr. Artaud to update your identification and portraitures. I am then to take you to Film and Television for an indoctrination video."

"Is Poppy attended to?"

"Yes. He is well taken care of."

"In that case," I say, looking at Ms. Lonesome.

"If you'll follow me."

"Yes, of course."

I follow Ms. Lonesome out of the kitchen, back down the western wing to the southern wing, through the offices of the clerical staff to the interoffice elevator bank.

Ms. Lonesome swipes her card. The elevator doors open. She steps in behind me and presses the button for the basement. The doors close. We descend. And I can't help but wonder what kind of indoctrination video.

"I understand that congratulations are in order, Mr. Louse," Ms. Lonesome says.

"Yes, thank you," I say nonchalantly, thinking that she too is referring to this error about my winning at Keno.

"For your trusteeship," she offers.

"You know of my trusteeship?"

"I was informed. Current trustees are entitled to know of new trustees. Current trustees are updated when new trustees are indoctrinated. All trustees have been informed."

"I see."

"I was updated first thing, when I reported to duty. Besides, I heard the celebration."

"But that was for some error regarding my winning a Keno game."

"It is a code for the ascension of a new trustee. Management believes a celebration is called for even though not all have a similar motivation for celebration. They informed the others that you had won at Keno."

"Yes, I see," I say, feeling a slight rush of blood come to my cheeks as I think of Ms. Lonesome's recognition of me.

The elevator rocks back and forth.

"I didn't know you were a trustee," I admit.

"There is no reason why you should have."

"I imagine not."

"You are no doubt pleased?" Ms. Lonesome asks.

"About you being a trustee?"

"No. About you being a trustee."

"It came as a surprise," I say, thinking of the great improbability, the numbers for and against me, thinking of Ms. Lonesome's strange and sudden candor, about her trustee status.

"Well deserved, I'm sure," she says. "Good fortune is always well deserved. You should be pleased. It is an honor." Ms. Lonesome looks at me in a manner she has never looked at me before. She is smiling. I have never seen her smile. Her eyes are fixed on mine. Her voice is more clear. Her words more pronounced.

"Yes, I am pleased. I see it as a great honor."

"A small step toward better fortune."

"Yes," I say.

"Yes," she says, smiling.

The elevator continues its descent.

My exchange with Ms. Lonesome has awakened me and settled my stomach. She and I now look up to the lit numbers blinking over the door, blinking my eyes shut as we fall through the teens. The rush of falling stirs Ms. Lonesome's fresh scent. I imagine the sweet coconut smell rising from her blouse, to the point that I can almost see the odor curling up her neck and wafting toward me, pulling me close to the thin line of shadow between her feet. I can see the brush of her hair on my toes, the shape of her thigh as it rests on mine, the curve of her chin as it hovers over me in midair...and her voice...

"Have they discussed your prospects for the future?" Ms. Lonesome asks as we exit the elevator. Her voice is most definitely clearer, stronger, more distinct. Her entire body, her presence, has become animate.

"I am aware of the positions I might potentially fill, yes," I say, wondering if this line of conversation is allowed. It must be if Ms. Lonesome is asking me such a question.

"Manager, middle manager, partner, etcetera," she says.

"Yes," I say.

"I have my sights set on manager, myself," she says as we turn a corner beyond Accounting and head down a hall I have never been in. It is a hall like a tunnel–white, beveled at the corners. And though I have never been here, there is something familiar about it.

"I am up for review next month. I am looking toward Intelligence. Intelligence is the future. Don't you think, Mr. Louse?"

"Yes," I say, hesitantly, having never really thought this for myself. "Intelligence is most definitely a worthy position. Dignified. Most definitely worthy of you, Ms. Lonesome."

"Thank you, Mr. Louse. That is very kind of you to say."

"Yes, very dignified."

Some color comes to Ms. Lonesome's cheeks and for some reason an image of her reflected in the same window I saw myself in earlier appears in my mind and then immediately disappears.

"Yes, well, Mr. Louse, they say it is a good time to be a trustee."

"Is that so?" I say, a little stupefied.

"From what I understand they are in the process of defusing Mr. Moorcraft's bombs and they have a strong lead on Mr. Blank. Paradise will be saved, and it's rumored there will be an Executive Lottery."

"Is that so?" I repeat stupidly, still trying to understand how quickly the situation has been resolved.

"They say they found a way to distract the Head Engineer and they have found a firm Controller who has helped them locate the missing funds and the source of Mr. Blank's sabotage."

"I see," I say.

I momentarily feel the relief. But then I begin thinking of Mr. Blank, or whomever it was I confronted in Poppy's chambers. I think of the way the man grabbed my arm and pulled me to the bed, the way Poppy's flesh felt against my skin, how the residue of sweat tattooed my palm.

Ms. Lonesome glances at me.

I glance away from her.

Then I'm distracted by the lights hanging from the corridor's ceiling. We pass one every few steps and I can see the intensity of their illumination left behind on my eyes. As we pass under their intermittent pulse I suddenly remember walking through a tunnel, a long, straight tunnel of bare earth and wooden support beams that stretches out as far as I can see. Caged construction lights dangle from wires hammered into rocks. I weave in and out of the beams and push against a strong breeze until the mouth of the passage opens wide and bright.

"Are you all right, Mr. Louse?" Ms. Lonesome asks.

I find that we have stopped and I'm leaning against a wall beside a set of double doors. The wave of nausea I felt earlier has returned and my head throbs at the sight of Ms. Lonesome's face. And the images don't stop. I can see the silhouetted claw of a bull-dozer and the neck of a crane, a morning light washing over the side of a hill into a valley.

"Are you all right?" Ms. Lonesome repeats.

"Yes, I'm fine," I say with some difficulty.

"Are you sure?"

"Yes, Ms. Lonesome, I'm sure."

Ms. Lonesome smiles at me with concern.

I remember the hot chalky smell of dry desert burn my nose and the back of my throat as I looked onto a silver starfish-of-a-building that shaded the land for miles. It rose hundreds of feet above the earth, and rested on immense metal pillars.

"I must be ready for my pharmaceutical, Ms. Lonesome," I say with my teeth clenched.

"Yes, Mr. Louse. That must be what it is," she agrees.

"Allow me just another moment if you will."

"Yes, of course."

Scores of wide craters surrounded the periphery and stretched into the distant plain of the desert, on whose horizon all I could make out were far away rock formations back-lit by the rising sun and a huge basin of dust that hovered above the ground like a low lying mist. I remember how the fine granules attached themselves to me as I walked down into the valley. I removed my jacket and wrapped the arms around my face so I could breathe freely. I cupped my hands over my eyes to avoid the spectacle of light reflecting off the glass and metal. When I reached the bottom of the hill I wandered around deep craters and swerved in and out of the shadows of the pillars. Triangles of metal crisscrossed under glass passages, making layers of kaleidoscopic patterns. I walked through the shimmering light and the dust until I found an elevator. The next thing I remember was being back in Poppy's secured zone. I went through the hall leading to Poppy's chambers. I passed a number of people whose faces I could see, but I don't recognize them, that is all but two, Ms. Berger and the woman who greeted me in Lounge 18 earlier.

"Please, Mr. Louse," Ms. Lonesome says, taking hold of my shoulder as she does Poppy's when he is ill. "Allow me to do something."

I shake my head at her.

I remember when I arrived in Poppy's chambers, the ceiling rose to the height of a cathedral's; it rose into a gigantic cupola, over which was the entire galaxy, the moon and the constellations on one side and the earth with all its colors on the other side. The only piece of furniture in the room was the bed. I could hear a woman say, "Who is that?" from one of the corridors. "Who is that?" I responded. A dark figure walked out as the sun began to rise over the earth. Ms. Lonesome emerged into the light. She said something I can't remember now. But I do remember that I walked toward her and my hands reached to her face.

"Please, Mr. Louse," Ms. Lonesome says, studying me. "Perhaps I should bring you to the infirmary, to Dr. Barnum."

"No, Ms. Lonesome, I'm fine," I whisper, looking at her crossly, recomposing myself, concentrating. I push myself from the wall and look deep into Ms. Lonesome's translucent eyes; all I can see are my hands reaching out to her face. As I stand up straight, the dizziness begins to pass.

"All right?" Ms. Lonesome says compassionately as she swipes her identification card for passage through the set of doors before us. I look at her carefully as she does this and wonder if what I see is a memory or a dream.

"Yes, I'm fine," I reassure her in a steadfast voice. "Really," I say, "perfectly fine."

"Good," she says, looking less concerned.

We enter and continue toward a waiting room where a very tall, skinny man with an oblong backside is standing against a glass panel of wall. He is in our standard uniform. A camera dangles by a strap from his bony hand.

"That is Glimmer Artaud. He will be photographing you. Good evening, Mr. Artaud," Ms. Lonesome says as we enter through the glass door.

"Ms. Lonesome," Mr. Artaud says is in a droll baritone, pronouncing her last name in two long syllables as if they were two words. His eyes are stationed at his upper lid. His face, like his body, is long and narrow. His jaw is unusually loose. His lower lip curls over his teeth as he affects what is supposed to be a smile, but isn't. His chin holds a deep cleft and dangles much like the camera in his hand.

"This is Herman Q. Louse, our newest trustee," Ms. Lonesome announces.

"Yes," he says, drolly, his eyes looking me up and down, but never leaving their stationary position. "Yes yes. This way."

Mr. Artaud leads the way through a swinging door and brings us into a circular room with a number of colored backdrops and some props.

"This way," he says, snapping his camera at me. "Navy, Mr. Louse. Navy."

My head circles the room in a blur of color, searching for navy as Ms. Lonesome takes a seat behind Mr. Artaud. I can't seem to take my eyes off her. I am still enticed by the image in my head. In a world in which I never expected anything to change, all of a sudden I feel something happening, something pulling me in directions I never imagined.

"Come, Mr. Louse. *Navy!* As in blue."

Mr. Artaud raises his eyebrows at me, then takes me by the shoulders and scoots me down to navy so that I am standing in front of a square of navy blue.

"Trustees go navy these days," Mr. Artaud exclaims to the ceiling as he removes a remote control from his jacket pocket. He clicks a button that turns on a set of very bright lights that blaze directly into my eyes. All the colors of the room are momentarily bleached out and little black dots begin dancing and melding onto the mucus of my retina.

"Navy! Say navy, Mr. Louse. Na-veyyy!" he sings a little vibrato. "Feel it in your lips."

"Na-vey!" I sing flatly, feeling my jaw drop and the corners of my mouth curling into the shape of Mr. Artaud's face, which doesn't suit me, but at the same time feels good simply because it is not my own.

Mr. Artaud clicks a picture.

"One more time, Mr. Louse," he says, stepping closer. "Na-vey!" he sings.

"Na-vey!" I say.

"Click," he says. "Na-vey!" he sings.

"Na-vey!" I say.

"Click," he says. "Na-vey!" he sings.

"Na-vey!" I say.

"Click," he says. "*Green!*" he sings.

"Green?!" I say.

"To the green backdrop, Mr. Louse," Mr. Artaud says, snapping his camera at me. "In the event that you become a manager we will have your picture on file. For the sake of expediency, efficiency, forward-thinking. We are thinking forward, Mr. Louse. For your benefit. For the benefit of all. Trustees think forward. Get used to it. Forward thinkers."

As Mr. Artaud continues his diatribe I search for green. But I am having a difficult time differentiating color after having all that light in my eyes. The black dots continue to dance and meld into breathing dollops.

"Green, Mr. Louse!" Mr. Artaud says firmly. He then pauses for my response. And then, "Ms. Lonesome! Would you please?"

Ms. Lonesome comes to my assistance. She swings me around and places me before the green backdrop.

"Thank you, Ms. Lonesome," I say, enjoying my close proximity to her.

"No problem at all. Come, Mr. Louse. Up."

She places her hand on the small of my back and holds it there forcefully. It seems that I have been bending forward in response to the sight of Mr. Artaud's concavity. Ms. Lonesome then lifts my chin in the direction of the camera and walks away.

"Don't move," she says.

"What did you say?"

"Don't move."

"That's what I thought you said."

"Don't move," she'd said. There's no reason why I should remember it. But she said it just this way.

"Give me green, Mr. Louse. *Manager green!*"

"Green Green!" I exclaim, lips pursed, thinking of how Ms. Lonesome had said, "Don't move."

"Not green green, Mr. Louse. Just one great big, *GREEN! MANAGER GREEN!*" he sings. "Open that mouth. Stretch those rose buds."

"Yes, all right," I say. The woman in SR-5 said it the same way–long on the "o" long on the "o." "Don't move." As I was about to get up. "Don't move." Long on the "o" long on the "o."

"Let me hear it, Mr. Louse!"

"*GREEN! MANAGER GREEN!*" I sing.

"Very good. Here we go."

Mr. Artaud presses the remote control and the blinding lights shine in my face.

"*GREEN! MANAGER GREEN!*" I nearly shout.

"Excellent, Mr. Louse." Mr. Artaud clicks the picture. "Red, Ms. Lonesome. Around to Red Middle Manager Red. Swallow the 'R,' feel the tongue in the back of the throat, hear the croak, looped like a boat on the bed of the mouth. Give me *RED*, Mr. Louse, *MIDDLE MANAGER RED!* Here come the lights."

The lights flash on.

"*RED*, Mr. Artaud. *MIDDLE MANAGER RED!*"

"That's the spirit, Mr. Louse. Now you're catching on. Click click. And onto gray with him Ms. Lonesome. Onto *GRAY!*"

"Onto gray, Mr. Artaud, onto gray," says Ms. Lonesome, concentrating on how to get me to gray.

I step in front of the gray backdrop and look into Ms. Lonesome's translucent eyes as she squares my shoulders. And what if it was her? What if it is her? What if she is one of them? Does that mean that I'm on her side or is she on mine?

"Come," Ms. Lonesome says. "This way, Mr. Louse. Look this way."

"Was it you?" I mumble.

"All right, Mr. Artaud," she announces.

"*GRAY PARTNER GRAY IS GREAT IN THE GRAY!*" bursts Mr. Artaud "Aaaand...here come the lights."

The lights flash on.

"*GRAY PARTNER GRAY IS GREAT IN THE GRAY*," I say.

Click click click.

"*AND ONTO THE DIRECTORIAL BOARD OF PEARLY WHITES!*"

Ms. Lonesome guides me across the room, one hand on my shoulder, one on my elbow.

"You shouldn't be letting your thoughts wander, Mr. Louse. Stay focused. Stay clear," she says. "Smile, Mr. Louse."

"Here come the lights, Mr. Louse."

Mr. Artaud points the remote control.

"AND ONTO THE DIRECTORIAL BOARD OF PEARLY WHITES!" I sing with as much enthusiasm as I can muster.

"Click click click," says Mr. Artaud as he clicks away.

My cheeks are contorted in spasms.

I open and stretch my mouth.

"And onto the finale, Mr. Louse. EXECUTIVE BLACK LOT-TERY BLACK WINNER WINNER WINNER BLACK!"

Mr. Artaud points.

"At the desk in the corner. Right there. You've got it."

I find my way to the desk in the corner. Ms. Lonesome wheels over the chair. It is the same desk as the one in Poppy's study. The same one at which he sits in a Transit Air promotion. With the same model airplane rising at a forty-five degree angle.

"EXECUTIVE BLACK LOTTERY BLACK WINNER WIN-NER WINNER BLACK, Mr. Louse!" Mr. Artaud positions his camera at his eye. "Give it to me," he says.

I begin thinking of Poppy in his chambers, in his bed with his bed sores, comatose, dying, and suddenly Mr. Artaud, with all his vibrant energy, looks like a piece of bent tinsel in the shape of a question mark. Simultaneously, the glow in Ms. Lonesome's face begins to fade and I have a sensation of euphoria as though whatever spirit once inhabited my body before my memory was annihilated has returned. I can feel what it is that has been lacking, but it is so mild and filled with riddles and confusions and is now, disturbingly, gone.

"Mr. Louse," says Mr. Artaud, slow and droll, brows raised, his momentum obviously broken.

"Mr. Artaud," I say, collecting myself, nodding my head. "I'm sorry."

Mr. Artaud flashes the lights.

"Executive black," I say, not smiling, not feeling like it. I look at Ms. Lonesome's dark profile as she stands next to Mr. Artaud and try to imagine the shape of her shoulders in my hands.

"Have it your way," says Mr. Artaud. "Click click click."

Mr. Artaud clicks away.

The lights dim.

"It's a wrap," Mr. Artaud says. "*Basta!*"

Mr. Artaud exits the room.

"Come, Mr. Louse," Ms. Lonesome says. We walk into the waiting room. We stand in silence. All I can think about is the darkness of the sex room. I try to listen for something familiar in my memory that would connect Ms. Lonesome's voice to the past. If it is her, is there a way that I could ask?

"Here we are," she says as my new ID is slipped through a mail slot. It falls into a small glass case. I pick it up. It is warm. Laminated. My bald head and large ears shine in contrast to the navy blue background. Written below, in bold black typeface, is:

HERMAN Q. LOUSE, TRUSTEE.

"Insert your old ID into the slot," Ms. Lonesome says, "and we'll be on our way."

I insert the old ID card into the mail slot, place the new ID in my pants pocket, and follow Ms. Lonesome out of the waiting room into the tunnel-like hall.

"On to Mr. Beeles," Ms. Lonesome says as we make our way down a corridor beyond the waiting area and Mr. Artaud's studio.

As we walk I occasionally look over at Ms. Lonesome, to the small flip of hair that bounces above her neck. And I can't help wonder why, if this dream that I have in my mind is a memory. What were we all doing there? Where were we? The more that I think of the other faces, the more I can tell they are nervous, as though they have been waiting for someone to arrive. I want to ask Ms. Lonesome if she shares these memories or dreams, but I'm afraid of how she might react.

The corridor ends. We come to a large metal door marked "Film and TV."

"Why don't you try your new card, Mr. Louse," Ms. Lonesome says.

I pull the identification from my pants pocket and swipe it through the electronic eye.

"Very good," Ms. Lonesome says.

As she watches me do this, I notice from the corner of my eye that she is looking at me with great pity, almost as though she sees something within me that I can't see; maybe it's that she knows something about me that I don't know.

I turn and look her in the eye as the door clicks open. But that look I thought I saw a moment before has disappeared.

She smiles.

"After you, Mr. Louse," she says.

We walk into a large room with rows and rows of televisions mounted on the wall and rows and rows of Film and TV staff wearing head phones, and who appear to be monitoring the screens, jotting down notes, programming. The images are mostly of scenes in the casinos, brought in by the closed circuit network. However, there are some films being viewed, including some of Dr. Barnum's old footage.

It is uncomfortably quiet.

A small, rail-thin man wearing glasses, a thick mustache, and a large pompadour approaches us. He carries a folder with large letters across the front: HERBERT HORATIO BLACKWELL: THE UNTOLD STORY.

"Hello, Ms. Lonesome," he says.

I recognize the voice.

"Hello, Mr. Beeles. This is Herman Q. Louse."

Mr. Beeles smiles.

"Mr. Louse, Mr. Beeles."

I smile.

"Yes, Mr. Louse," Mr. Beeles says. "Nice to finally meet face to face."

"Yes," I say, looking more closely at his folder. "It's a pleasure."

We shake hands.

"Just making preparations for the inevitable," he says, holding up his folder. "The inevitable's inevitable. Don't let anyone tell you otherwise."

Mr. Beeles lets out the laugh of a showman.

"Mr. Louse is our newest trustee," Ms. Lonesome says. "Coming directly from the wings."

"A new trustee? Well, nice to have you aboard, Mr. Louse. It's an exciting time for us trustees."

"That's what I understand," I say.

"If you'll just follow me, Mr. Louse."

I turn to Ms. Lonesome.

"I'll be returning to my duties now, Mr. Louse. I trust you can find your way back."

"Yes, of course," I say, feeling an emptiness at the thought of her leaving me.

"Well then," Ms. Lonesome says.

"Well then," I say. "Good evening."

"Good evening," she says. "Good evening, Mr. Beeles."

"Good evening, Ms. Lonesome."

Ms. Lonesome looks at me for a moment. She blinks her eyes, then exits through the door we just entered.

"If you'll just come this way, Mr. Louse, I'll show you to your screening room."

Mr. Beeles walks us by all the glowing monitors into a wide corridor that leads past a number of doors. He takes me to the very last one on the left.

"This is an indoctrination room," he says as he opens the door and turns on the light.

The room isn't exactly a room, but rather a booth with a television monitor and a chair with a bucket seat and wide armrests. A pair of headphones hang from the ceiling.

I step in and sit down in the deep seat.

"What you're about to see, Mr. Louse," Mr. Beeles continues as he leans against the door, "is a video especially designed for new trustees. It is meant to be a learning tool to help guide you through the rules and regulations that govern a trustee. You will find that, by virtue of the fact that you have become a trustee, you will be granted certain liberties at specific times in specific places, all of which are much too complicated to explain in a brief sitting. This screening will be the first of thirty-six thirty-minute installments.

Tomorrow, and for the thirty-four days following, you will come to us every morning to view the subsequent segments of the tape. Is that clear, Mr. Louse?"

"Yes, Mr. Beeles," I say.

"In that case, I'll let you alone. The headphones are above. You can adjust the sound and the resolution of the screen with the remote control on the armrest there."

"Thank you," I say.

"Very well then," Mr. Beeles says as he shuts the door. "Good viewing."

The door clicks closed.

The television monitor turns from black to blue. As I place my headphones over my ears the logo of G. appears on the screen, the silhouette of the skyscraper eclipsing the setting sun.

Mr. Bender steps out from behind a burgundy velvet curtain into a spotlight.

"Welcome to Trustee Indoctrination Tape Number One. First allow me to congratulate you on your progress. Making the leap from future trustee to trustee is a monumental achievement. To have made it to this level, you have without a doubt, in the eyes of the Executive Controlling Partner, in the eyes of the organization, in the eyes of fortune, proven yourself worthy to take on the forward-thinking, forward-reaching, forward-moving position of trustee. Such an opportunity is rare and should be cherished and held in the highest regard by new trustees. I say this first and foremost because the position of trustee is a position of earned privilege, not, I repeat, not a position of entitlement. The position of trustee can and will be taken away if the individual holding this privileged position acts outside the parameters of behavior allowed trustees. In order to sketch out acceptable responses, actions, inquiries, gestures, and general interactions with staff members, we will be spending the next thirty-five sessions rehearsing conversations, considering hypothetical situations, and making comparisons and contrasts between the life of the future trustee and the trustee. We will try to find what behaviors you have learned acting out your duties as future trustee which you can apply to your new position as trustee. We will discuss incentive systems designed to increase a trustee's probability of moving into the position of manager, middle manager, partner, etcetera. I will explain the system of analytical reviews, which will be examined by our in-house specialists to determine where your talents as a trustee might be best applied. We will consider the long-term payment options a debtor-trustee is privileged to choose between, and how these options compare to those of the future trustee and the manager, middle manager, partner, etcetera, etcetera. We will carry out tests designed to…"

Mr. Bender's voice is monotonous and begins to lull me to sleep. As hard as I search for some small bit of information to keep me stimulated, I can't. All of sudden, as if a bird has silently swept down from the sky and flown just inches from my face, I can see in my mind the man who visited Poppy's chambers earlier, the intruder I have been ordered to disregard, sitting in front of a wall of monitors just like those in Film and TV. He observes all the various floors of G., including Mr. Sherwood's and Dr. Barnum's offices, Dr. Barnum's sound stage, Poppy's chambers. On other monitors I can see images of the desert, where men and tractors break ground and where cranes sit in pieces waiting to be assembled. However, this is all I can remember of this scene. The images fade and I can't see any more and am left to wonder if I'm making it all up from bits and pieces of things I've learned. The essence of my memory materializes and dematerializes as quickly as I'm sure that what I am seeing is real.

Mr. Bender has moved to the other side of the stage.

"The long-term advantages of being a trustee should provide the proper incentives for a trustee to maintain a healthful perspective and optimistic outlook on his daily activities. Consider the alternative to being a trustee. Consider the lifestyle of the future trustee compared to the trustee. The trustee is a privileged member of the Resort Town of G. The trustee is almost assured a seat in Paradise; whereas the future trustee still must earn the potential assurance to Paradise. Paradise does not await just anyone. Paradise is more than a conceptual predisposition to good fortune for the trustee. The trustee must understand, first and foremost, his role in constructing Paradise; whereas the future trustee has yet to understand the tools with which we are to journey forth to Paradise. We are about to embark on an evolutionary time. As a trustee you will help shape the milieu that will be looked upon by future generations as an age of enlightenment. As a trustee you will act as an arbiter of this enlightenment, a…"

• • •

I remember the others more and more. And there were others! There were others in the structure where I touched Ms. Lonesome's face, others in the room, the one with the window, in which I had been seeing my reflection all evening. There, in that space, I can see them standing around talking to one another, more casually, without looking fearful, looking onto the open view of the desert. And now that I think of their faces I know I have seen, here in G., more than just Ms. Lonesome, Ms. Berger, and the administrator of Lounge 18. There are a number of faces in my mind right now that feel like words on the tip of my tongue, but for some reason I can't recall any names or when we met or why we were together. I do recall, however unrelated, riding in an elevator with Mr. Godmeyer, who, paying no attention to me, looked up to the display as the numbers climbed to eighteen, at which floor we exited and were met by three men. For some reason I tried to run from them. But without considering any human formalities—for instance, to allow me the option of force or cooperation—the three of them lifted me off the ground and carried me over their shoulders. They opened a door, walked me into a room, and wouldn't let me down. I screamed at one of the men who was tying me to a chair with straps for my hands, feet, and neck, and a headrest for my head. The chair reclined back so my eyes were several feet from the doors of a large cabinet. Another man placed a contraption on my head that looked like a pair of blinders a jockey would put on his horse. Another man bolted the chair to the floor and opened the cabinet doors to reveal a very big TV. The TV was on, and on the screen was an image of myself, my face. It was me placing bets and losing money and placing bets and losing money. As I watched this, I remember I couldn't see the bets I placed. I could only see my face—the distress and the pleasure from losing and winning. I remember I sat there for what felt like weeks. They came and went with food and allowed me to wash in the mornings and the evenings. I got so sick of my own image and so sick of looking at the greens and reds of the casino. However, this was only the beginning. Eventually they started playing the same hands and bets for hours at a time, then another and another, day in and day out—blackjack, craps, poker, baccarat, roulette. I couldn't tell how long this went on, because I couldn't see the time and the drapes were drawn and the lights were on. Hundreds of bets were rerun hundreds of times until it made me physically ill. I remember wanting to reach out and kill those who were causing me that pain and suffering. I remember fixing my vision on the pixels of the television screen. One by one they told somewhat cartoonish stories of their own about boys and girls and sex and love. I saw desert sunsets and desert springs and cactus blooms and fields of saguaros and open farmland. There were redwoods and sequoias and mountain switchbacks and panoramas of birds flying in flocks over wetlands. A lightless sky full of the Milky Way blanketed still waters. Shadows of furious eucalyptus caught in a hurricane. Wildfires burned chaparral hills. Bullets pierced sunflower petals. A woman and a young boy tended to a garden of narcissus bulbs and irises and danced as free as the fragrance made them feel. When those attending to me removed my soiled clothes and led me to the bathroom, the disorientation, as excruciatingly dizzy as it was, was filled with the same beautiful imagery. As we walked the vertiginous walk I saw blossoms flowering in the attendants' hairs. Each follicle and bud contained the eyes of spring and breathed the sounds of the casino. Holding onto their shoulders, looking at their heads, each strand of hair mimicked the voices of the patrons, the losers. Everything I could read from the repetition of events on the television was relived with human contact. When they held me up in the shower, the marble stall filled with eerie silences and feet shuffling, with nervous contained laughter, distant sounds of slots being pulled, wheels spinning, bells of the winners ringing and the groans of the losers losing and the pensive clicking of chips of those pacing themselves for another day. And with all this, the smells of the tables would come to me and suddenly the soap smelled like cigars and alcohol and sweat and perfume. When the henchmen dressed me, their finger nails only reflected the beautiful hands I'd been dreaming of— flushes and straight flushes and royal flushes and four of a kind aces and full houses of kings and queens. When they strapped me back in with the buckles clasping and the big television filled with an image of my hands throwing cards to a dealer with a lisp and an oversized bow tie, I could see more than the formality of the hand I was holding and the fate that accompanied the hand. I could feel the process of each motion in my body and feel the coming illness that accompanied the repetition. Each motion was like a finger crawling into and down my throat to start the entire process over again. That moment when the attendants came and carried me to the bathroom to be cleaned—each time it took what seemed to be longer and longer. They played each of my hands that many more times, and when it finally reached the point of absolute absurdity, I started blacking out, eyes opened wide and rolled into the back of my head, memory lapsing and searching for where I was and why I was there. It was almost like having a concussion but without the blow to cause it. My mind with the absence of beauty collapsed on itself and left blank tape unraveling. It was somewhere at this point that I started waking up to the vision of this awkward-looking man I have now seen in Poppy's chambers and the same one I've seen sitting before the monitors. I remember finding his face and smile pleasant, and surprisingly, all the images that accompanied my other experiences didn't reflect on his teeth, in his eyes, his hair. He had an aura about him that he was untouchable and pure and I was delighted to find that I could look him in the face and not find part of my wretched self. He was truly beautiful to me, a vision not unlike that of Adam touching the hand of God in the Sistine Chapel. I was elated to find him there every time I came to. Every time I came to, he stood there longer and longer but never said anything. One time when I was in the shower, I asked an attendant who he was, but the attendant denied that the man existed and said I was hallucinating. But the man continued to come and stand before me. Then one day he spoke and said we would be meeting together in the near future when my life would be changed for the better.

Before I know it, the audio of the television cuts off, Mr. Bender dissolves, and the television fades to blue. With that, an image of the skyscraper eclipsing the setting sun returns to the screen, and the screen turns black. I look into the void, staring at the pale glimmer of my distorted reflection.

Mr. Beeles opens the door.

"Let me show you the way out, Mr. Louse," he says.

"Yes, thank you."

I get up from my seat and walk out into the hall feeling disoriented.

Mr. Beeles closes the door behind me.

"I hope you found that informative."

"Yes, very."

"See you tomorrow. Same time."

"Yes," I say. "Tomorrow."

Mr. Beeles walks me past the wall of television monitors. He opens the entrance and deposits me into the hall.

"Until tomorrow, then."

"Until tomorrow."

AIRS DOCUME

WRITTEN CONFESSION OF MORTIMER BLANK –/–/– 3:49:57 A.M.:

Where do I begin? I turned away from my wife as she softly said things and cried things and asked me questions I couldn't answer. Some hours later, I found myself driving on the interstate away from her. I trailed in the wake of a semi that rocked my small car back and forth. I was shaken far into the middle of the night until I reached the outskirts of the City of R. where I came across a flashing neon sign for the Queen of Spades Motel. The parking lot was empty. It was lit by the Queen's sad yellow eyes and the rest of her royal vestiges. Her red robe was faded pink, her golden tiara flickered like a dusty tin can, and the neon surrounding the spades in the corners had escaped, turning the inverted black hearts into large black holes. The letters T E QU E O S ADE M T L pulsated one word after the other into the sky and onto the barren landscape.

• • •

A nicely shaped woman in a strapless red velvet dress walked across the parking lot. The neon lights shimmered off the velvet and the sheen of her blond hair. She held heels in her hands and walked barefoot across the asphalt. Her figure became darkened and then disappeared when she swung open the door to the casino. The casino was a one-story shoe-box-of-a-building with a boulder facade framing green plate glass windows. The light from inside cast a green glow onto the parking lot and onto the dust and moths that hovered around a large wagon wheel hanging over the front entrance. The wheel silently rocked back and forth in the night's gentle breeze.

I parked my car. When I reached the casino's entrance, a few figures in cowboy hats shadowed past the window and I could hear, "Let's get some reeeed roses / For a / Bluuuue lady…" I stepped inside to find a feeble place with tattered brown carpeting and faded green craps and roulette tables run by a couple of old sleepy-looking men. The woman in the red strapless dress sat on a stool in front of a row of slot machines. She wasn't playing. She was just staring at a stained glass mosaic of horses grazing beside a generic wagon train. For the most part, the bulbs backlighting the glass panels had burnt out, and where they hadn't, around the tails of the horses and the heads of the wagoneers, gnats and moths circled. I sat down next to the woman, reached into my pocket, and held out a dollar coin. "Go ahead," I said. She turned her head and looked me over, as I did her. She had put her shoes back on and was gently scratching her heel with the point of her toe. As she looked at me she bit at her lower lip. "You broke?" she asked. I looked into her eyes, which were a translucent blue and full of curiosity. "Yeah," I said, feeling as tattered as the carpeting at my feet. "Me, too," she said. She smiled and nonchalantly slipped the dollar into the slot. She graciously offered the handle to me with her arm extended and fingers splayed. I pulled the handle down and let it go. Together we watched the wheels quickly and then slowly turn and turn until they clicked into place. To my astonishment each wheel stopped on 7. For the longest time, the machine sounded with bells and clinks of metal. A few of the cowboys came by with "gosh darns" and "god damns" and left before the machine paid out. She and I sat there silently, both of us stuck within our own thoughts. When the machine finally spit out its last dollar, we just stared at all the silver coins, and stared some more. And then we looked each other over again. "Would you like to take a ride with me?" I asked. "I know where to go," she said. "So do I," I said. "G.?" she asked. "How did you know?" I replied.

It turned out the two of us had received the same brochure on the same day the week before. We got in my car and drove through the City of R. We drove onto the interstate through the long desert valley and at around dawn we exited onto a narrow road leading to G. When we arrived, we parked the car in the vast lot circling the tower and immediately went to the roulette tables. We and thousands of others stood under the giant chandeliers at the center of the casino where dozens of silver balls simultaneously spun on their tracks. Everything we played for hours on end came easily to us. We played until one of the hosts approached us and offered us a complimentary suite in the VIP wing. We took it, showered, had a nice meal—we did all the things you're supposed to do when you win. When we woke up, we got dressed and went directly to the blackjack table. As these things so often work out, however, our mood had changed, the way we looked at each other had changed. It was apparent to the both of us that together, for the time being, we were losers. Recognizing this, we amiably parted company and continued on alone. I don't know what became of her. All I know is that shortly thereafter all my money, with the exception of a few hundred dollars I still had left on my wife's credit card, was stacked up and lost. At this point, however, something extraordinary occurred. A man in a gray flannel suit approached me and took me aside. His name was Quarry. He said he had been watching me play the day before and he told me that his luck was down. He asked if I'd play with his money if he offered me a share. "Of course," I said. He handed over a tray of chips and we journeyed forth into the gambler's tale of the up and down suspense variety, with one exception: As I stood there losing Quarry's money, Quarry didn't really care. In fact, he seemed to take pleasure in my losing his money. I'd look over my shoulder, and there he was with an innocuous grin on his face without one crooked line suggesting the slightest bit of regret or malice, nothing. He didn't even watch what bets I put down. Yet, at the same time, I could feel a host of eyes observing my actions. And with that, I was able to catch myself long enough to give Quarry back his money and move toward the front door to the cashier, where I took out the cash advance on my wife's credit card. Quarry was perfectly satisfied with my decision and let me go, except he started following me from table to table placing the same bets I placed. This went on for several hours until I lost everything again. Quarry continued to reach into his pockets and pulled out chips, offering them to me. It was at this point I realized that he started resembling...I don't know what to call it. He had the confident gestures of a benevolent benefactor but he didn't seem to be acting out his own will. This scared me, and suddenly I felt guilty and longed for the comfort of my family. I said good-bye and thanks to Quarry for the opportunity and walked away from him, getting as far as the slot machines at the front entrance. I shadowed him from across the room, and then he saw me. There was no space-age beaming, just a glare in his eyes. I felt a preternatural force pull my body and lift it off the ground, dragging it toward him like the deadened flesh of a zombie. I took the chips rising up from his palms and he wished me good fortune from the innermost recesses of what I perceived as goodness. I thanked Quarry with a tone of gratitude and an inward-looking eye staring down my detestable nature. Together we walked to the craps table, and with Quarry's hand on my shoulder I started placing bets.

THE CONTROL

I walk back through the hall, pass Mr. Artaud's studio, thinking of that moment in my new memory when I reach out to touch Ms. Lonesome's face. She, like the others, has fear in her eyes, and I can feel myself afraid as well. I remember us trying to find our way out, after searching for a door; the door was supposed to lead us to someone who was going to transport us away or to some form of transportation we could use to escape. We were escaping. I remember them saying to me, and I saying to them, that we should devise a plan and hide if we can, somewhere within, but as we sat and discussed this it was too late. We heard the sound of shoes echoing through the metallic halls. There were many feet approaching quickly from all directions. And before we knew it, Mr. Bender and Mr. Godmeyer and their men began pulling us away one by one.

I exit the hall in front of Accounting. The hall is bustling as the staff changes over to the morning shift. I check my watch. It is six o'clock. The swing shift accountants walk in pairs to the elevator bank as the morning accountants walk past them. Low murmurs of "Good Morning" vibrate off the glass panels that border the hall. I stand up against the glass, waiting for the throng to dissipate before

I attempt to make my way to the elevator. I stand before a huddle of three as they intermingle, exchanging the morning news.

"They're saying the Executive Controlling Partner is dying."

"He's been implicated as well, you know."

"It's to be expected now that he's on his way out."

"All those who die are always implicated."

"He would have it no other way."

"They're saying that he's the one behind Moorcraft and Blank."

"No, that's old news, the new news is that he is Moorcraft."

"No, that was false news. They are saying that Moorcraft never existed. He was invented by Blank."

"That is new news."

"He was a fiction to test the wills of those involved."

"Which makes Blank...Moorcraft?"

"Yes."

"Who else could it have been?"

"He did a very good job."

"The best."

"In any case, G. is saved from destruction. The bombs have been dismantled."

"It is therefore the best form of news."

"Without a doubt."

"The Executive will go down in the best possible light."

"He will never hear a bad word to make him turn in the grave."

"He's a stalwart."

"A man of the people."

"Well deserving of a burial in Paradise."

"I hope to visit him there one day."

"My greatest aspiration."

"They're expecting the lottery as early as noon."

"That means there's going to be a drawing."

"What a thrill it would be to visit him wearing his own epaulets."

"It will be the first drawing ever."

"Very exciting."

"Exciting indeed."

"Thrilling, in fact."

"I don't know what I would do if I won."

"I wonder what happens to the winner."

"It must be good."

"It must be great."

"It must be better."

"Why else would they go through with it?"

"Because it's the best system in the world."

"None better."

"Indeed. The most civilized."

"Thank God we're trustees."

"The chances aren't so bad."

"The percentages are in our favor."

"I'll be thinking of your good fortune."

"And I, yours."

"Same here."

"Good fortune."

"Good fortune."

"Good fortune."

And the huddle breaks up. Two walk away. One walks in. I stand alone, feeling an awkward and sincere melancholy at the news of Poppy's impending death, but now am confused as to why I feel this way. And who is making this news of Moorcraft not existing, that he's Poppy, that he's Blank? If not by the name of Moorcraft, he most definitely exists. How could Dr. Barnum and Mr. Sherwood be so horribly mistaken?

"Mr. Louse?" I hear behind me.

I turn around. A midget with fat hands and an oversized forehead stands, half in, half out a door.

"Yes?" I ask, recognizing his face from my memory. I remember searching a stairwell and a number of corridors with him as we tried to find a way to escape from Bender and Godmeyer.

"Ah, what good fortune," he says in a surprisingly deep voice. It is the voice of a large man. "Such good fortune. I was told you would be down here."

I approach him as the accountants continue to pass and take their seats, face their computer screens, rest their hands on their keyboards. I notice, to my surprise, that many of the faces, like this midget's, are familiar to me. And all of a sudden I feel as though everything of my past is catching up to me at once, whether I want it to or not.

"Lumpit," the dwarf says, holding out his small hand. "Walter Lumpit. I was told you were on your way out. And here you are."

He smiles as I shake his little hand. His fat cheeks bulge and quiver.

"Good morning, Mr. Lumpit. What can I do for you?" I ask appropriately, knowing full well that I am following through with whatever destiny holds. I follow Mr. Lumpit toward his office, between the glass walls that comprise the other offices, where every so often I notice an accountant passed out cold on top of his or her desk. Mr. Lumpit doesn't pay it any mind; therefore I don't either, not feeling safe to assume anything and feeling sympathetic to their dilemma, being recently guilty of this negligence myself.

"I understand congratulations are in order," says Mr. Lumpit as he steps toward his desk.

"Yes. I imagine so." Mr. Lumpit is strangely calm for a man who is one of the accused. Unless he is no longer accused. Perhaps his status has changed?

"Congratulations then."

"Thank you," I say.

Mr. Lumpit's desk is one third the height of any other desk in the office but has the same surface area. He stands up on his chair and leans across the desk for a pad of paper.

"I have been asked to prepare your portfolio so that I can brief you on your financial status later in the week," Mr. Lumpit says. "As a new trustee you have several payment options you didn't have in the past."

"I see," I reply as Mr. Lumpit picks up a pen as big as his torso.

"Yes," he says. "It's really quite liberating, in fact. Fines, fees, new debitures can be quickly eradicated with a healthy cost containment plan. Not to mention the reduced interest rates and the volunteer programs we have set aside as incentives. You might think of consolidating, or funneling future time into futures in the organization. As a trustee as opposed to a future trustee, as you learned from the video this morning, you may use time as collateral to buy shares. G. is doing very well these days. Very well indeed. Futures are a healthy start for a forward thinker such as yourself, Mr. Louse."

"Yes, indeed," I say.

"In any case," Mr. Lumpit says, "I just wanted to make sure that everything is in order. Your ID number, Mr. Louse?"

"Four, nine, four, five, seven, nine, zero, nine, nine."

"Very good." Mr. Lumpit writes the number on the pad and then jabs his little finger at the computer keyboard.

"It's really a very exciting time for you," Mr. Lumpit says, smiling as the information instantaneously comes up on the screen. "The future is only a small step away in the life of us trustees. It is closer than we would ever expect. As the Executive says, 'Time can only be captured by those willing to capture it. The end of the future is the beginning of the past. There is no middle passage. There is no time like the present.'"

Mr. Lumpit continues to smile. I'm not sure what to make of him, other than that he is familiar to me. However, his smile is somewhat knowing and more than a little nervous. As Mr. Lumpit continues to smile, I notice through the corner of my eye that there is a quiet commotion taking place directly behind me.

I turn for a better view.

Mr. Bender stands at the door of an office. He is pointing at one of the accountants, one of those I recognize, a young woman with frizzy hair and an expressionless face. She slowly walks to Mr. Bender. Mr. Bender directs her to the hall where there are five other accountants standing beside Mr. Godmeyer, who is carefully placing heavy shackles on their legs and arms. I feel a shutter run up my back as I feel the synchronicity of events.

I turn to Mr. Lumpit. He is still smiling, his cheeks quivering.

"And you realize that you are eligible for the drawing, Mr. Louse."

"I am aware of that, Mr. Lumpit."

"Yes, ever since Mr. Moorcraft became Mr. Blank and G. was saved from destruction, it is safe to say the drawing can be at any time now."

"Yes, I'm aware of that, Mr. Lumpit."

"I'm glad that you're aware of that, Mr. Louse. Please be advised that this will be of great concern to you," he says, smiling as though what he is saying carries a greater weight than I could possibly know.

"Yes, Mr. Lumpit."

"Yes, Mr. Louse," he says seriously.

"I'm afraid I don't understand."

"I don't mean to disturb you, Mr. Louse. I am simply saying that caution befits a new trustee as well as cunning."

Mr. Lumpit motions toward me.

"My final duty, Mr. Louse, just so you know, is to you. In that sense it is for the both of us. Keep that in mind as you proceed."

Mr. Lumpit looks around a little and then looks back at me.

"Like you I have been allowed to remember little things. I have been informed of little things as well. For your safe passage, of course. The little things make big things don't they, Mr. Louse?"

"Yes, Mr. Lumpit," I say. "Little things make big things." And I realize that although I don't really understand what is happening, Mr. Lumpit is undoubtedly placing me into some kind of jeopardy.

"I'm glad you agree, Mr. Louse. Well, here is my little thing. For you, Mr. Louse, I have passage to a familiar place," he says gravely as he taps away at his computer. "Ah, here we go, Mr. Louse," he says as the monitor changes color and presents some kind of financial document. Mr. Lumpit presses a button. The screen changes. And then all of a sudden Mr. Lumpit's expression becomes ponderous.

"It seems that a trip to the Controller is necessary, Mr. Louse. Certain developments," he says, still considering the information on the screen.

"Excuse me," I say, as I continue to watch Mr. Bender do his rounds. One of the accountants is cowering in the corner of his office. Mr. Bender walks after him, takes him by the arm, twists the man's arm around his back, and leads him into the hall.

"An impossibility," Mr. Lumpit says, acting a little distracted, as though he finally acknowledges the arrests taking place around us. "At least an improbability. A mix-up."

"I don't understand," I say.

"According to this file it shows that there are two Herman Q. Louses with two different files with two different sets of data, with several ID numbers."

Mr. Godmeyer is now placing black hoods on the heads of those accountants he has already shackled. When I look back to Mr. Lumpit, he rests his tiny chin into his tiny hands.

"There're no two ways about it, Mr. Louse. I'm afraid I'm going to have to send you to the Controller to straighten this out."

"Whatever you think is best, Mr. Lumpit."

"Most definitely, the Controller. This way, Mr. Louse."

I follow Mr. Lumpit out of his glass encased cubicle down the hall to an interoffice elevator bank. He presses the button of the elevator.

"Ninth floor," Mr. Lumpit says. "Room nine-eleven. Best of fortune to you. Once again, congratulations."

Mr. Lumpit says all this smiling, cheeks bulging and quivering nervously.

"Be careful, Mr. Louse."

Mr. Lumpit walks back to his office. As he arrives, Mr. Bender approaches him and leads him to the hall. He is the last one, making it an even dozen. Mr. Godmeyer cuffs his wrists and ankles and places the oversized black hood over his head. Mr. Bender walks out and takes the front. Mr. Godmeyer takes the back. And then off they march through the hall until they drift out of sight.

The elevator arrives.

I step in and punch the ninth floor.

The doors close and I ride up.

When the elevator doors spread apart, a man falls toward me into the elevator and makes a tremendous thud as he drops onto his left shoulder and then onto his face. I bend down and turn him over. I place my cheek against his mouth and find that he's breathing. His skin is warm. The fat arteries in his neck pulse ever so slightly.

"Excuse me," I say as I gently tap his cheek.

The elevator doors close onto his shins and bounce back open.

"Are you going to come to?"

I tap at his cheek again, this time a little harder. He is a man of medium height and wide proportions. He has thick brown eyebrows, a pockmarked face, and a permanent dimple shaped like an asterisk on the lower part of his jaw.

"Sir?" I say again as the doors close and bounce back. I dig my hands underneath his shoulders and pull him out of the elevator into the wing, where I notice there are a half dozen other men and women passed out on the floor in various contorted poses, sparsely and evenly scattered to the end of the corridor. I drag the man in my arms out of harm's way and lean him against the wall under the elevator control panel. As I stand up from placing him in as comfortable a position as I can possibly arrange, a thin woman with straight auburn hair and narrow arching eyes walks out from the office closest to the elevator.

"Excuse me," she says appropriately.

"Excuse me," I say as I step back. "Would you happen to have any news about this?" I wave my hand at the unconscious bodies in the hall.

The woman presses the "Down" button to the elevator and turns back to look at the bodies. She yawns as though she is about to answer me, or is at least considering my question, and then drops forward as her eyes disengage from consciousness and roll up toward the top of her head. To her good fortune, she falls directly into my arms. I pull her close and drag her over to the door from which she just came.

I walk down the hall toward nine-eleven, making my way around the sprawled bodies. I have never been to the ninth floor. It is similar to most other floors: transparent glass walls, white doors, beige floors, a popcorn ceiling, an internal labyrinth of offices recessing to the periphery of the building. As I walk down I notice that there are many others inside who are passed out cold on top of their desks, on their phones and computer keyboards, on the floors, in the aisles, sitting upright in chairs, teetering to one side or the other. Those who are still conscious act as though nothing has happened. They continue their duties in the manner they are accustomed, pushing aside those who are in the way as necessity dictates.

I step over a man's arm and turn left into room nine-eleven. I open the door and follow my way, straight and then left, through a glass-paned hall that deposits me at the front desk, at which, to my utter surprise, is Ms. Florence Berger. She is sitting upright in her chair, staring directly at me with her neck rigidly upright and her head angled forty-five degrees over her right shoulder. Like Mr. Sherwood's receptionist, Ms. Berger sits with one hand folded over the other on top of a green blotter. When I step up to the desk, she delicately replaces one hand for the other.

"Herman Q. Louse to see the Controller," I say, not mentioning Ms. Berger's name in order to spare her the humiliation of her thinking that I know who she is.

Ms. Berger just stares at my chest and moves her head from one shoulder to the other. Her green eyes are bloodshot and glassy. Her lips are tightly pressed together so that I can hear her breathing through her nose, and I can't help but think of the arrows of water darting away from her when she was in the tank. I don't remember Ms. Berger as well as I do Mr. Lumpit. I merely have an image of passing her and looking at her talk to a balding man with thin eyebrows.

I wait a moment longer for Ms. Berger to respond. When she doesn't, I walk back toward an office enclosed by oak walls, assuming, I think safely, that this is the Controller's office. On my way there I find that everyone in this department has fallen over in the same state as those in the hall, all except one man who is gray at the temples and who is intermittently bouncing his fist against his knee after vigorously scrubbing his computer screen with a white cloth, in order, it seems, to stay awake.

"You won't find him in there," the man announces as I continue toward the Controller's office.

"Where is he?"

"Arrested. Some say conspiracy, some say for his relationship with the Executive Controlling Partner, some say for money laundering, some say for mishandling records, some say for all of the above. He was mischievous. Very mischievous. I dare say he has what's coming to him."

And with that, the man very vigorously bounces his fist on his knee. He punches hard, hitting, but to no avail. And then as spontaneously as the woman began to fade back near the elevator, the man yawns and slowly slinks off his chair, under his desk into a ball.

I sniff the air in search of an unusual scent, thinking that it might have something to do with an escaped gas. But all I can smell is ammonia, as fresh and pungent as it always smells wherever I happen to be in G. Its smell is so ever-present I can hardly even smell it until I close my eyes and think about it hard enough.

When I open my eyes, I find that Ms. Berger has gotten up from her desk and is now standing next to me.

"If you will please follow me, Mr. Louse," Ms. Berger says in a barely audible monotone. Her eyes are no more alive than when I arrived. Her lips move without any indication that the rest of her face knows that she has just spoken.

I don't even feel compelled to ask her why or on whose orders. I must have faith that whatever it is that's guiding me has some greater intelligence. I allow Ms. Berger to walk ahead. I follow her slow, soft movements back to the oak walls of the Controller's office.

"If you'll just swipe your card through the sensor, Mr. Louse," Ms. Berger says.

"Yes," I say, not knowing why I should, but somehow knowing it will work. I am obviously here for a particular reason.

I swipe my new trustee card through the sensor device. The door clicks open and swings in.

Ms. Berger and I slowly follow it and allow the door to automatically close behind us. The office is the exact image of Mr. Sherwood's office only smaller, more compact, with no windows. The man outside who informed me that the Controller had been taken away was mistaken or was living through an hallucination when he watched him being hauled off. For the Controller, who turns out to be Mr. Hamilton, my former collections official, is here, reclining back in his leather chair, passed out like the others.

Ms. Berger wheels him off to the side, into the back of the room against a wall of bookshelves filled with ledgers and other books full of what look like rules and regulations and other such things. When she returns to the desk, she steps before the computer terminal.

"May I please have your identification card, Mr. Louse?" she asks as she holds out her hand.

"Yes, of course," I say and hand her the card over the desk.

She runs the card through a small black box next to the computer and then looks at the monitor. I walk around to the other side of the desk to see what she is seeing, to find five rows of numbers scrolling up the screen. When the numbers are through scrolling, Ms. Berger hands my card back to me and then lifts the lid of another black box, larger and more rectangular than the first.

"If you'll just place your hand over the screen, Mr. Louse," she says, holding open the lid.

"Yes," I say, and place my hand on the screen. As I do, the screen reacts with a thin bar of light that slowly and laboriously travels up and then down the box, all the time illuminating the veins, arteries, and bones under my skin. When it is through I can see an imprint of my hand and crooked thumb on the computer monitor. Ms. Berger closes the lid to the black box and presses "Enter" on the keyboard. More numbers begin scrolling. Ms. Berger and I watch the screen until the last rows trail up the blue background of the monitor. And when this happens, a nine digit code blinks and flashes.

Ms. Berger writes this code on a piece of paper and then hands it to me.

"Please be careful with this," she says, and then begins walking out of the Controller's office.

I place the piece of paper in my coat pocket and follow Ms. Berger back to the outer cubicles. Once again, I allow Ms. Berger to walk ahead. And once again, I follow her slow, soft movements, this time toward the elevator, thinking of the metal around her wrists and ankles and the way her thin naked body looked through the refracted lights in the water, how she reacted with such ferocity and loathing at times and how it now reminds me of her face in the halls as we heard the approaching footsteps.

When the elevator arrives Ms. Berger and I step into the shiny silver interior of the chamber. She presses floor eighteen. The elevator slightly rocks back and forth and pulls up on our legs, bending my knees. Ms. Berger stands stiff with her disengaged eyes fixed on the door. The sight of her sunken cheeks and the paleness of her skin makes my stomach turn sour. Her face is innocent at the moment. Even if she were imperfectly human at some other time, she is now perfectly innocent and devoid of spirit. It is as if she is hardly breathing.

When the doors open, the sight in the hall is no different than that of the ninth floor, with the exception of several more bodies sprawled about. I allow Ms. Berger to step ahead of me. As before, I follow her down the hall, around the bodies to another glass paned vestibule. I can't help but wonder what purpose the code serves. Part of me cares, part of me doesn't care. I will hand it over gladly.

We turn right and then left as we zigzag into the back of the building where we enter a secured zone, the Internal Affairs Records Department. There is no one conscious around.

As we reach the very back of the building, near the windows we walk into an area containing an extensive series of floor-to-ceiling filing cabinets. We occasionally step over a passed out body or two; some are piled on top of one another. Ms. Berger doesn't pay them any mind. She walks robotically to an aisle, opens up a file drawer, and removes a black leather briefcase. She shuts the drawer and hands the bag to me. She then pulls out a shelf built into the filing cabinet and presents it to me with an open palm.

"You have what you need, Mr. Louse," she says dispassionately.

"Thank you," I say.

"Good fortune," she says, and squarely walks off through the corridor, turns right, and disappears.

Without any hesitation I rest the briefcase on the shelf and open it. Inside is a thick stack of papers on top of which is a note.

Mr. Louse,
You are to briefly review this document then deliver it to the thirtieth floor via the interoffice elevator.

I don't know where to begin reviewing such a monstrous body of work. I flip through to find transcriptions and summaries of transcriptions and turn back to the very first page.

Mortimer Blank, formerly of the city of K., arrived in the resort town of G. at 5:47 A.M.

Some months after losing his job at the Law Offices of Yangdon, Font, and Barthelme he was targeted by Outreach Services, who initially spotted his record on a search of default accounts. They followed up by sending brochures about our credit guarantees. Mr. Blank called and requested further information and then sent credit reports and references.

Mr. Blank is on the verge of bankruptcy and has tapped all available resources. Other than his estranged wife and son, he has no living relatives. Mr. Blank's misfortune stems from gambling problems and bad employment decisions. All employers with whom he had found jobs consistently followed recent downsizing trends, thus leaving him laid off with no eligibility to collect unemployment (as his positions only lasted several months at a time).

I flip through several more pages, and notice a yellow tab toward the back that I didn't notice before. I open to this page.

WRITTEN CONFESSION OF MORTIMER BLANK −/−/− 4:30:33 A.M.:

When I had gambled away a substantial amount of Quarry's money, and after we had stayed up for two days straight, Quarry disappeared while I dozed off on a bar stool. When I woke up, the bartender was staring at me. "I was told to tell you when you woke up that the man you were with has cleared it with the management to issue you a line of credit." The husky voiced bartender pointed me to a dealer who stepped up to an open table. The dealer stared at me until I lifted myself up from the stool and followed his eyes. "You have an open line of credit for twenty-four hours, Mr. Blank," he said. I signed for fifty thousand to start. I signed for fifty thousand more five hours later, and eventually, another fifty thousand. The banks' boxes opened and closed, my eyes fixed on the credit slips as they stuffed them in. At times, on that day, I questioned if it wasn't all an hallucination. I thought such thoughts as I greedily roamed the floor until I landed in the very center of the room, where I was interrupted by an insipid looking man with hands, head, legs, and feet too small for his torso. He was dressed in the same kind of gray flannel suit Quarry was dressed in, and he asked me if he could have a moment. I, of course, agreed, seeing that he had all my signed credit vouchers and it had just turned the twenty-four hour mark on my line of credit. He said something to the effect that it was time and that he would need to discuss arrangements for payment with me. I said I was under the impression that this was all paid for. I told him about Quarry. He smiled a pugnacious smile and told me that Quarry had merely vouched for me and said that I was good for whatever debt I incurred. That was very gracious of Quarry, I said, and I went on to say that it was a simple misunderstanding. "I'm afraid not," he said, holding up the vouchers in his hands. "There is over two hundred and fifty thousand dollars of debt here. You have incurred two hundred fifty thousand dollars of debt, Mr. Blank." You can imagine what was going through my mind at the time. Or maybe you can't. It doesn't really matter. "Got your nose" is what he was saying in a very administrative manner. We were standing near the cashier when it happened, that is when I saw her pass, the security guard, whose holster just happened to be undone. The strap of leather that fastened her gun was flapping back and forth with the motion of her wide hips. There wasn't a conscious decision to do what I did; it just happened as though my body knew much better than my mind as to what was right for me at that moment and there needn't be any rational reconciliation between the two. I didn't think. I lunged. I lunged for the gun and easily took hold of it. And as though my fingers knew what was right I pointed the gun at the security guard and then at myself, at my head as I faced off with the woman and then the pit boss standing near the little man in the gray flannel suit and I can't remember what I did next. I swung the gun back and forth demanding this and that until someone larger than I am pounced on my body and everything went black.

Mortimer Blank. As hard as I try to associate that name with myself, I can't. But it is undeniably my story. With all else in my head, I can't see any of what Mortimer Blank has described. But I know it is my story. I saw it on the television when Mr. Bender and Mr. Godmeyer greeted me. Yet I don't remember putting the gun to my head, the image of it traveling to my temple or the feeling of its metal touching my skin. Mortimer Blank. I don't remember. Mortimer Blank. I can't say it to myself enough times to jar it loose from all the images breaking free in my mind. Mortimer Blank. Me? And what if it's true? If I am Mortimer Blank, am I the Mortimer Blank who has caused all of this confusion? Can it possibly be me they are searching for?

My thoughts are so crowded I'm surprised I have room to think words. The images move so quickly I don't even know if I can accurately describe any of what's before me. The images repeat themselves over and again, as if to surface once isn't enough. And I can see all of it is beautiful and interesting to look at but I am unable to appreciate any of it because it all flashes by so quickly that I can only feel the short pulse of its rhythm.

I close the file and the briefcase. I latch it shut and try not to think of what to believe. I don't wish to think at all. I want to turn it off. I walk down the corridor, straight and then to the right, between the glass walls, and I count numbers to try to erase the fragmented visions and the confusion that accompanies them.

I am nothing I know of and my stomach is nauseated and my head is in pain and I'm full of exhaustion and all I really want is to return to my quarters for my pharmaceutical. I want this all to end. I will do anything to make it end.

I accidentally step on the leg of a man and then the hand of a woman, and I look at my own hands and wonder what it is I am made of and why I have arrived at this moment in time in the middle of all this as I have. Is it God's cruel joke? To hide my consciousness as he has? To let it be played with in such a perverse fashion? Should any animal have to endure such uncertainty in one given time?

I approach the elevator.
The doors open without my having to push any buttons.
I step in and ride.

19. IN A HOT, DARK GLOVE COMPARTMENT SOMEWHERE OUTSIDE THE RESORT TOWN OF G.

RESORT TOWN

Dearest Associates,

After falling back to earth, you undoubtedly have a number of questions about what has happened and what to do. Your questions will be answered in time as your memory returns and as your personalities realign themselves. I expect, however, that you will be fragile for some time, since you have been through a particularly difficult experience. I have provided you with a map and some money and directions to find the few people you left behind some years ago. I can't promise they will welcome you with open arms, but there is always the possibility they will comfort you through your initial endeavors. I mostly write this to you as a form of confession, a story, if you will, to try to justify what I have done, as I'm afraid that in the final moments I will not have the time to explain myself.

To begin with, as each of you will be aware at this point, I betrayed your trust in order to benefit my future. You will come to remember that I promised to help you escape, but what was really to be your escape attempt was only a momentary diversion. It is true that I initially rescued you from your indoctrinations, but, really, I only delayed them. I took you from your rooms and enabled you to escape from G.; I moved you into the valley to Paradise, where you believed you would eventually be free.

All of this was necessary in order to complete the plot, which you now embody from your experience. I don't believe I have been an evil person as much as I have been driven to this desperate act. I don't imagine you will ever feel that my selfish motives benefited us all; but this is true.

Like yourselves, I have been held captive here and was taken from my life as you were taken from yours. Many years ago I lived near the foothills of N., where I worked for an architectural firm and led a quiet life. One morning when I arrived at the office, I found a letter in my mail box from a Ronald Sherwood. The letter said that I should meet him at the Golden Trails Restaurant in the local train station to discuss a business proposal. Naturally my curiosity was piqued, since I didn't know who this man was at the time and nothing as remotely interesting as this had ever happened to me. I wasn't one of these dashing young architects with a mane of hair and a trophy wife dreaming of buildings with my name etched in their marble facades. I didn't think twice about going. I drove out to the train station at the specified time and took a seat at the counter of the restaurant. Mr. Sherwood approached me from a back corner table, and without asking if I was who I was he introduced himself, then requested that I take a walk with him.

We walked out through the train station and onto one of the platforms, talking in generalities of N.'s inhospitable surroundings. Mr. Sherwood told me that he was representing a party who wished to hire me and that this party was waiting for us on the train. I thought it a little peculiar but didn't see any reason not to meet with him. When I agreed, we boarded an empty car and walked to a closed door at the back of the caboose. Mr. Sherwood knocked and told me to wait a moment while he announced me. I stood there admiring how immaculately clean everything was — from the floor to the windows to the ceiling — and how distinctly it smelled of antiseptic. The light was dampened by dark tinted windows, but I could still see there wasn't a speck of dust trailing through the air as you would usually find in an enclosed space like this. All the seats had been gutted in every car and every car was sparsely decorated with expensive furniture whose seat covers and cushions were covered in plastic. Moreover, there was no one to be seen throughout the entire train. I started to feel a little strange about being there. My imagination was starting to recognize the oddness of the setting. I, who had always been naturally predisposed to laugh a good, hearty laugh in the face of a peculiar situation, became uncharacteristically afraid of the awkwardness of the moment. I thought of leaving, but as Mr. Sherwood opened the door and told me that I could go in, my reflex was to follow. He placed his hand around my shoulder and escorted me through to the other side. As I walked into the caboose, Herbert Horatio Blackwell, whose face I recognized from the newspapers, sat before me at his desk. He was well groomed, his nails and his hair were short, his face clean shaven, his trademark pencil-thin mustache immaculately sculpted. He was dressed in a bathrobe. An ascot ribboned around his neck and funneled the smoke rising from the cigarette between his fingers. I looked at him, then at Mr. Sherwood, and then at him again, thinking of his celebrity and my insignificance, and true to my awkward nature I began to laugh. The laugh, unfortunately wasn't the slightest bit contagious. It erupted in silence and bounced off their two stern faces. Mr. Blackwell, ignoring my outburst and thus declaring his distaste for my reaction, told me to have a seat. I sat down in front of his desk and watched his eyes survey me. He told me of his plans to build a gaming center at a location he wouldn't disclose, and asked if I would be interested in acting as his head architect. He told me that he was aware of my qualifications, knew exactly who I was and what I was capable of. In other words, this was not a case of mistaken identity. He was willing to pay me more money than I ever had dreamed of making. But I had to decide immediately. The train is leaving in five minutes, he said. It's up to you. He ashed his cigarette into the gold ash tray resting against his knuckle. Once again, I looked at Mr. Blackwell. I looked at Mr. Sherwood. I looked at him. And I laughed, not nervously as I should have, but as gregariously as I had at first. This was no indication of what I was feeling because I was undoubtedly nervous; unfortunately, this expresses what was and more than likely still is my pathetic ineptness at social grace. When Mr. Blackwell and Mr. Sherwood, once again, didn't react, didn't let up from what I thought was a ruse, I sat there dumbfounded. For about two of the five minutes I remained dumbfounded. Then I thought about it for the remaining three as we sat in silence. And then I nodded my head and said, "Yes," as the train departed. I nodded some more and laughed some more, this time nervously, as the two men continued their silence and stood coldly by as I humiliated myself in front of them. We traveled across the country, back and forth along the northern route, and then back and forth again along the southern, while Mr. Blackwell met with me about his plans. The plans slowly revealed themselves as we talked, but what also slowly revealed itself to me was the relationship Mr. Blackwell had with my mother while he was at the decline of his celebrity as a movie maker. I learned that the two of them had had an affair and that when my mother became pregnant she ran off to N. At this, I didn't laugh. At this, he laughed. But after this he never laughed again in my presence. Mr. Blackwell kept track of me as I had grown up and he felt that now was the time to claim me as his own since I had a skill that could benefit him and our future together. I tried to see the whole thing as a great adventure at first. I tried to admire Mr. Blackwell as my father, as a celebrity, as my employer. However, as the months passed, I began to learn how truly strange he was and how it was too late for me to turn back. I had become his possession, as it were, the symbol that represented his legacy should he ever be struck ill, which, in his thoughts, could happen at any time. I was constantly watched by a guardian whose job was to make sure I played my role dutifully and that I was doing my job properly. Since the day I arrived at the location that would eventually become G., since the day I learned that I was his, all I've wanted was to leave. However, from the moment I nodded my head at the train station, this was never an option. It was never a topic to be discussed. As Mr. Blackwell's son, I was to listen obediently and help him plan our future. I have spent many years here, trapped on the thirtieth floor in my workshop, designing his vision of Paradise. I know it appears that I have had liberties and power, enough of both to act out in some manner, but I assure you this hasn't always been the case. It has only been a recent development, all due to a whimsical moment in Mr. Blackwell's life and only with his express authority. What has been done today, ironically enough, has been done by him, for reasons I can only say are mysterious. What I have done has been a direct expression of his will. The outcome of the situation has been an extension of his morality. I wish I could grant you and all the others more than he has; however, his will is his will and it must be seen to its final conclusion. I wish you the best of fortune.

Yours sincerely,
Herman Q. Louse
Head Engineer

20. THE PRODIGAL SON

THE PRODIGA

The elevator opens onto a small entry that leads to a narrow corridor. There are no intercoms and no one is present. The only presence is the red blinking lights of the surveillance cameras. I step into the entryway, and as I do the elevator doors close. I walk down the hall. After a short distance I turn a corner that leads me to a door marked "Contents of 747 Romaine," the name of the vault from which they say they retrieved all the names of the accused. I try the door, but find that I am unable to open it. I tug a few times and realize it is impossible. When I give up I turn around to see, on the opposite side of the corridor, a few feet down, a large green metal door marked room 3033, which is open a crack. I step down to it, take hold of the handle, and gently pull the door toward me.

A storage room stretches out as far and wide as the Great Hall. The walls and the ceiling are made of industrial gray steel and the space is cluttered with an amalgamation of wood scraps, machinery and tools, plastic tubes, drafting tables. The room is sectioned by walls of all this stuff and much more. Mazelike passages of discarded junk lead to both the right and the left and wind around to places I can't see.

"Hello!" I call out.

No one responds.

I wander off to the right and begin winding around one of these passages. It leads me into an area in which I recognize many objects similar to those I know I have seen in Poppy's study. There are rolls of old Asian rugs stacked into pyramids, and sofas and chairs piled on top of each other. Marble statues with broken arms and legs lean against other marble statues. Severed marble heads are strewn about the floor along with shattered watches whose inner coils and springs prick out like coarse ingrown hairs. They make a path to a line of coat racks covered in white sport coats, double-breasted suits, and robes with the monogram HHB on the chests. Piled to the side of the coat racks is a huge mound of brittle-looking leather flight jackets covered in dust. Beside this are broken-down wheels, rusted propellers, and wing fragments of an old plane, as well as instrument panels and other cockpit gadgets. I step over dozens of trampled Stetson hats and find, against the wall, a sail boat's mast that reaches as high as the ceiling; it rests beside old golf clubs and mortar shells pointing upward, and piles of defused grenades and trundles of a tank. Leaning against stacks and stacks of yellow legal pads are posters promoting EKG Productions and Transit Air; one of which showcases a young Poppy sitting at his large desk with a model airplane. There are old movie projectors, cameras and screens, movie facade doorways to old buildings, more posters of such things as satellites and rockets and space shuttles lifting off in front of large bodies of water. There are framed news clips captioned "Einstein at Manhattan Project," "Allied Forces storm the beaches of Normandy," "Roosevelt, Churchill and Stalin in Yalta," "Mushroom cloud over

Hiroshima," "Oppenheimer before Congress," "MacArthur on the move," "MacNamara on the front," "Armstrong: 'One small step for man...'"

I weave in and out of these things, trying not to step on anything, realizing that it is all familiar and realizing why the objects in the study always felt familiar. It was more than just my daily trips to deliver Madame's butterflies. It was more that I knew of these things intimately, of these things and this place.

"Hello!" I call out again. I turn another corner into a new passage where I'm confronted with three full length portraits of Jane, Kathryn, and Betty. Unlike the holograms in the bathrooms that only reveal their upper torsos, these extend to their feet, where at the base of each, in gold stenciled letters, it reads "Jane Kathryn Betty Blackwell." They all stand at the same height. Their hands, though slightly aging a little more in each of the paintings, are the same shape. I now see their resemblance, in the broad ovals of the eyes and the cheeks, and for some reason I know that this was Mr. Blackwell's mother; I now feel foolish that I couldn't even recognize them as being the same person. If I think hard enough I can remember these features in my memories of Poppy's younger faces. If I extract the light and the feminine qualities, they are there, broadened and proportioned to suit the face of a man. I feel dumb that I haven't lifted the shadow of this earlier. It's been before me the entire time, calling attention to itself, if I could only see.

"Hello?!" I call out again.

Still no one responds.

"What would you have me do?!"

I slowly wind my way back through a passage in which I have to walk over old black and white photographs. They are dull and yellowing at the edges. Some are of overcast oil fields full of Eiffel Tower–shaped derricks. But mostly they are of Poppy as a young man. I stop momentarily at a picture of him in a tuxedo. He is at a party, encircled by women in low-cut dresses. Dr. Barnum stands in a corner balefully staring down into a martini glass. I work my way down the passage, tiptoeing over images of sports cars and parades, Poppy dressed in leather flight jacket, ascot, and goggles. And then, one of Poppy sitting in a wheelchair beside a crashed plane. His legs are extended in casts, his arms bandaged. He is looking away from the camera, squinting at the horizon. I see sticking out from under this photograph, something that momentarily makes my heart stop. It is the image of the view I initially saw in my memory when I hummed the melody in Poppy's study. A white sun spreads over a dark tinted window that reveals small areas of mountainous terrain. I hastily kick the picture of the crippled Poppy aside to find an image of the man I saw in Poppy's chambers sitting in an ornate plastic-covered chair looking out the window of a train. And I remember seeing the same view as I drove in my car off the highway when I first arrived at G. Over his shoulder, in the corner of the image, is the profile of Dr. Barnum smoking a cigar. Reflected in the window is an image of Mr. Sherwood with a camera that covers half his face.

I turn another corner and come face to face with a mannequin cloaked in Madame's black dress and veil. I nearly knock it over as I make the discovery. The hands are plastic, the eyes missing, the entire thing a rigid artifice. I touch the material of the dress and feel its silky texture.

Behind the mannequin's head is a thin burgundy sheet hanging from two hooks on the wall. It ripples against the current of the air conditioner. As the bottom corners sway and flap up a little, my temples begin to swell and I can feel some anxiety spread through my chest. For I realize where I'm standing.

I walk past several more mannequins to the nearby wall and pull the sheet from the hooks. Before it wafts to the ground, I can suddenly see the corners of tinted glass. When the material falls to my feet, I find myself staring at my reflection in the window. As in my memory, the scrim isn't down; it is never down. The window reflects the small frame of my body. I walk toward the glass until my reflection is large and wide and dissolves into the expanse of desert outside. A hair-thin line of lavender light outlines the distant rock formations on the horizon.

I used to stand here. I used to stand here with the man and watch his face in the window, his and others, just before sunrise. Although he never said what he was thinking I knew he was dreaming of leaving this place. And I... I was here because he wanted me here, me and the others.

I walk back across the workshop, through the maze. I pass the mannequins and the portraits and go to an old wing of a plane leaning lengthwise against a wall where a narrow passage leads to another large room with stark white walls. Several human-sized models of what look like space stations are mounted at the center of the floor. They rise up on beams that are stationed on what looks like a merry-go-round. The models are made of wood, Styrofoam, and clear plastic tubing, through which I can see small figurines tending to gardens and computer terminals, communing at meals in large banquet halls. Figures are suspended in midair dressed in space suits. Each of the structures spins slowly. Their central points face a giant wheel of fortune suspended from the room's high ceiling. The wheel of fortune spins as well, and as I step under it, it casts a breeze onto the top of my head.

I notice that each station is named: Jane, Kathryn, and Betty. At the base of it is a flimsy sign reading "Paradise Beyond Paradise." As I get closer I can see there is a miniature facsimile of Poppy's chambers set within the center of each module. His chambers are exactly the same, though instead of tin foil on the windows there are pictures of space, the moon and the earth on either side, the same constellations I can see from the skylight in my quarters.

The closer I look at each model I find that there's even a small figurine for the attendant in the corner, and a television monitor at the foot of the bed. There are three corridors leading to small space ships; and another three corridors leading to his bathrooms. There are miniature facsimiles of the bathrooms as well. Jane Kathryn Betty Blackwell glows above the sinks and faces the toilets. They are perfect little replicas of the holograms.

"Hello, Mr. Blank," I hear.

"Mr. Blank," I say as I hear it. I look at the briefcase in my hand, then look at the door beyond the models from where the voice is coming.

Standing in its threshold is…

"Hello, Mr. Louse," I say without thinking, surprised that I am saying this, but knowing that it is his name, that I have had his name, Herman Q. Louse. Mortimer Blank, I think to myself, Mortimer Blank, and try to remember.

I walk around to the other side of the stations, taking notice of all the small, intricate gadgets working together to make them spin and coexist on the same geometric plane. It looks like a solitary universe unto itself, one into which I wish I could jump, to hide, to disappear.

"Would you mind giving me that piece of paper in your pocket?" he nearly mumbles.

"No, not at all." I reach into my pocket, hand him the piece of paper, and am happy to be rid of it.

He carefully looks at the paper and sticks it into his pocket.

All of a sudden I can hear a man's voice coming from behind the door, from behind Mr. Louse.

"Bring them this way," the voice says. "Stand against the wall. We'll be taking your statements shortly."

I move closer to the door, to the man I knew as the intruder. The silent fuzz of a low level static hovers as I observe him standing before me. His sandy blond hair is brushed out of his eyes and is combed back above his forehead. He looks at me and then looks over my head to the models.

"You remember me now?" he asks.

"Yes," I say.

"In a way I was hoping you wouldn't just yet," he confesses, looking shamefully down at his shoes. "I suppose you remember who you are and how you arrived here as well?"

"Yes, somewhat," I say. There is part of me that wonders why he is seeking this conversation with me. But I can see he is ashamed. Or so it appears.

"And how are you feeling in general, physically?"

"Nauseated," I say.

"It will diminish," he assures me. "Sooner than later."

"I don't understand. What is it that's making me feel this way?"

"You're going through withdrawal. You and the others. You've been injecting yourself with a placebo for the past several nights. That's why you've begun to remember."

All I can think of is how my last dose of pharmaceutical made me feel dizzy in its usual way. I wonder when I finally remember who I am if the veracity of my own character will be anything worth being proud of.

"Has all the scandal been over this?" I ask, pointing back to Paradise Beyond Paradise, looking upon it with Mr. Louse.

"In some ways, yes. In some ways, no."

"Will you tell me?"

"Yes, I'll tell you everything I can in a minute, Mr. Blank."

"Good," I say, "because I want to know."

"Come along, Mortimer," he says as he takes me by the arm and pulls me through a vault-like door into the hall. He locks the door behind him. We walk through a long, dark, and narrow corridor filled with mirrors and glass museum cabinets overflowing with Poppy's paper planes. The planes are piled on top of one another like molting moths. I can't help but wonder what the repercussion will be when all those people lining the halls and the offices awaken and remember everything from square one.

We pass more and more mirrors and my image begins to multiply, as does Herman's. We walk toward an open shaft of light that distorts our images, doubling them from what they just were.

"I said not to move!" a voice bellows.

"I didn't move. She moved."

"I didn't move. He moved."

"I didn't move. She moved."

"Enough already. Mr. Blurd, you're first!"

And there is a loud clanking sound, followed by clomping shoes and a series of heavy thuds. We step through the light into darkness, where I notice we are standing inside the large office with the wall full of monitors similar to that of Film and TV. The sounds I have been hearing are coming from the Accountants' interrogation. They are now lying on top of each other, passed out, with the hoods over their heads. Their interrogator has fallen down as well. The only one standing is poor Mr. Lumpit who keeps walking against the walls and cursing his ill fate.

Otherwise, I can see much of G. on the other screens. It is at rest. Hundreds of piles of people in the wings, a rebroadcast of Ms. Berger's correction playing to a sleeping audience in the Great Hall, the motionless gaming room, Mr. Lutherford and Mr. Heinrik lying on top of Ms. Morris in the kitchen, Mr. Crane asleep on his bed, his neck stretching toward the peep hole into my quarters where Mr. Bender has fallen over my desk. Dr. Barnum and Mr. Sherwood sit slumped at Mr. Sherwood's office desk, their necks craned forward, their mouths open. Poppy looks blissful as he lays prostrate in his bed. Ms. Lonesome is there in the chambers. I notice she has rolled his wheelchair up beside the western night table and laid out a set of clothes.

Mr. Louse turns and faces the wall of monitors and looks back at me, then goes to the monitors, touches a button, and watches all the screens go black. He then leads me back into the hall of mirrors. When we've walked a few steps he turns me around to face a mirror, to face my face and his face simultaneously. I look closely at mine, trying to make it mean something, thinking of the briefcase in my hand and what it contains. All I can think of, however, is that Mr. Louse, though obviously fully capable of administering all this mischief, appears somewhat simpleminded.

"So then, I'm Mortimer Blank and you're Herman Q. Louse," I say, sounding and still feeling somewhat mystified as to how this came to me in the manner it did.

"Yes," he says.

"Mortimer Blank," I repeat, trying to get used to the sound of the name.

"Yes," he repeats.

"But why did I have your identity?"

"Because Poppy requested it."

"Why?"

"In all honesty, I don't know," he says, looking as bewildered as I feel. "In all honesty, I've never understood how his mind works. But if we really thought about it, you and I, I would imagine for the same reason Madame visits his chambers once a night."

"I don't understand."

"For starters, Madame is Poppy's mother."

"But Poppy's mother is dead a long time already."

"It isn't really his mother. It's Helga Zimmerwitz, the receptionist in Lounge Eighteen SR-Five."

"The receptionist in Lounge Eighteen SR-Five?"

"It is part of her duty to play Madame."

"Helga Zimmerwitz is Madame."

"Yes, Madame. Like you're me, she's her—the symbolic representation of Poppy's mother."

"As I'm the representation of you?"

"Yes."

"And who are you to be so important to be represented?"

"Poppy's son."

"Oh," I say. I look Herman over more carefully, weighing the fact that this is Poppy's son.

"I can't say this for certain, but by taking the name of Poppy's son you provided him a certain fantasy of having his son attending to him."

"But I look nothing like you."

"I imagine it has nothing to do with that."

"But why me?"

"I don't know," he says shrugging his shoulders. "If I had to guess, because he felt you were the best person predisposed to do what you've done."

"And that would be what?"

"Arriving here with this piece of paper," he says, tapping his pocket with his bloated hand, looking at the pocket, looking at me.

"Why would he be interested in having you obtain that?"

"It's part of the plot."

"Which part of the plot?"

"The part of the plot that follows his assisted suicide."

I sigh at the thought of it, sigh at the thought of my part in it.

"Part of the plot was that he wished to die; and in the process of dying he wanted to be sure that I took what he believed belongs to me and doesn't belong to Mr. Sherwood or Dr. Barnum, or anyone else for that matter."

"And so the number on that piece of paper represents your inheritance."

"It is a code to a bank account on the tropical island of Z."

"The tropical island of Z.?"

"Yes, located in the Gulf of R."

"To which you'll go after Poppy's dead."

"That's what he wishes."

"But tell me something."

"What?"

"I thought his entire purpose was to live. His ultimate purpose is to live."

"Again, I really don't know," he says, shaking his head. "I mean, perhaps. That's all I can say. I can't really say. I've never really been very good at understanding him entirely."

"But all the precautions, all the compulsions, all the minutiae, are they not the signs of his will to live?"

"I mean, maybe there is death and then there's dying. It could be he's unafraid of death because he's already achieved infamy. With infamy, he'll remain immortal. To die is another thing. To die one must allow for one's final deterioration. This, until now, I don't know that he's ever accepted. Now, maybe he's accepted it. Had a change of heart, a revelation, or something to that effect."

"A man like Herbert Horatio Blackwell has a fleeting change of heart, a revelation."

"Like I said, I don't know. I can't begin to understand him. All I know is that one day while Helga Zimmerwitz knelt before him, he handed her my first orders and I have followed them one after the other with the hope that this would all come to some kind of end."

"So you and Helga Zimmerwitz devised a plan to kill him."

"No, Poppy devised the plan to have himself killed. Poppy has devised all the plans. All the plans involving yourself and the others. From the very beginning. From the very day you arrived. This has been planned for a very long time. It's taken a very long time. Do you realize, I've been here for, I don't know how long, but ever since I have been here he has been planning, threatening to plan something like this. It's only now that he's gotten around to it. I mean, the codes alone. Do you know how long it took him to encrypt the codes so that I could move them through the computers without detection?"

Mr. Louse bites at one of his fingernails.

I shake my head. "I don't understand," I say.

"As you've been giving Poppy a gradual overdose of Librium over the last several months, breaking him down bit by bit, I have been feeding codes into the computer, hiding the finances, re-arranging them, you see?"

"No, I don't see."

"This whole business regarding Paradise Beyond Paradise?"

"Yes?"

"Well, Paradise, was simply an expansion of G., only more elaborate, more complex, more populous, more contemporary. But Paradise Beyond Paradise, now that was to be cutting edge. I anonymously sent Sherwood and Barnum doctored books of finances and diagrams and convinced them that the conspiracy was taking place with all of those who have been arrested in the past several days. But in reality, there is no Paradise Beyond Paradise, just the idea of Paradise Beyond Paradise, in order to get them to believe that the great amount of money that has disappeared has disappeared. I mean, wouldn't you believe it?"

"I did."

"You see. But they eventually began to catch on. Sherwood figured out that there was the slightest possibility that the whole thing was a deception and that the funds hadn't left G. at all."

"Which is the truth?"

"Which is the truth. That's why Poppy ordered me to plant the bombs. For the likelihood they should figure this out, which he considered very likely, and which he, for the most part, planned."

"Then there were bombs?"

"Yes. Mr. Moorcraft's bombs. My bombs. One and the same."

"But now they have dismantled them."

"It gave them something to do. It gave them a sense of accomplishment. It was at this point that Poppy ordered you to inject his lethal dosage of Librium, which Barnum and Sherwood happily observed from the monitors in Sherwood's office. They believed Poppy was killing himself before they could do as they pleased with him. Now, with Poppy dying, Mr. Sherwood, pleased as punch, invited you to join him in his office in order to make you a trustee."

"But for what purpose? They had what they wanted. What could I give them that they didn't already have?"

"Herman Q. Louse. They needed Herman Q. Louse, his name, face, and body to retrieve the floating finances."

"But I thought I was Mortimer Blank."

"You are Mortimer Blank, Mortimer," Herman says as he takes a breath. "But, before you became Mortimer Blank again, you were still Herman Q. Louse, and Herman Q. Louse retains the rights to the Executive Lottery."

"Retains the rights? I don't understand 'Retains the rights'?"

"In other words, the man designated as Herman Q. Louse retains the rights to the Executive Controlling Partnership of the Resort Town of G."

"Which means?"

"In reality, there is no Executive Lottery. Herman Q. Louse is Poppy's son and Herman Q. Louse inherits the Executiveship. All the lawyers would say so. All the lawyers would insist. They were made to believe this. They believe this. All the lawyers together have power whether they know it or not."

"So then, what you're saying is that they were planning to swap me for you."

"So if I were ever to come out to claim what's mine..."

"They would do away with you and be left with me?"

"Their puppet."

"Their pawn," I say, wondering whose puppet I would rather be, wondering what exactly I have worked toward.

"That's why you became a trustee last night."

And now I can partially see what he's getting at.

"To make me eligible for the Executive Lottery."

"Precisely."

"But, if you don't mind my saying so, why should Herman Q. Louse win the Executive Lottery if the Executive Lottery is open to all trustees?"

"As I said, because I'm the executor and all the lawyers say so and therefore..."

"The Executive Lottery really *doesn't* exist."

"Exactly. The Executive Lottery doesn't exist. The computer says so. Intelligence says so. All the lawyers say so. Pan Opticon says so. Barnum and Sherwood say so."

"But if everyone believes it exists, doesn't it exist?"

"Yes, until Pan Opticon changes the news and then, you know..."

"It no longer exists."

"That's just how it is."

"Nothing is absolute."

"No need for revolutions, upheavals, etcetera. But you know what? It doesn't matter any longer. None of it really mattered to begin with."

"And why not?"

"Because Poppy had them all drugged while you were drugging him."

"Them?"

"Yes, Sherwood and Barnum were drugged by Bender and Godmeyer, and Bender and Godmeyer were drugged by Sherwood and Barnum."

"Drugged?"

"Yes, drugged dead. Once and for all. Poppy managed to set the two against the two with rumors and reports within their own ranks."

"Dead?"

"Yes, dead."

"And the others? All the others?"

"No no no. Only Barnum and Sherwood, Godmeyer and Bender, and some others in Internal Affairs and Intelligence, Detentions, Sales. No no no, the others are going through withdrawal."

"Like me?"

"Only you started sooner. It was planned that way."

"Then why bother with all the rest of this?"

"If I knew I would tell you. Probably, if I had to guess—to keep me preoccupied."

"And that would be enough of a reason?"

"Everything is enough of a reason."

"In any case, you were saying earlier about the codes. Why me and the others and the codes?"

"The codes? They've been circulating through the system, hidden in various places at various points in time. That's why Poppy needed the others, you see. You and the others, when you were admitted to G., each of you were encrypted with a series of internal codes. But before you were moved from admittance to indoctrination, all of you mysteriously disappeared from your quarters and some days later reappeared in the wings of Paradise."

Herman looks away as I think about what he's saying and understand the significance of it. And I can see myself walking through the desert under the giant structure; I can see us huddling in the wings.

"While you and the others," Herman continues uncomfortably, "had apparently escaped, your numerical codes hung in limbo long enough so that I could assign the new encrypted codes to your internal documents. This way when you returned I would be able to shuffle the funds from one to the other through the Controller's office, in which Poppy always assigned one of you, one of the ones with the proper code."

"Why wouldn't he allow you to control the Controller's office?"

"For the same reason I couldn't control the Controller's office from here. Poppy was afraid I would make a blunder or take the money prematurely, foil his plans. Oh, he couldn't stand it if he were foiled. And it is for this reason that you became a trustee tonight. You see?"

"No, I still don't see."

"He substituted you for me in the computer and tried to replace your codes at that time so that when the money finally came to you they could trace it back to me."

"Why couldn't you just substitute it back?"

"I just couldn't. I wasn't able. The Controller who was controlled by Poppy had it locked up."

"Which left you where?"

"Between me and you. If I wanted what I wanted I needed you, Herman Q. Louse, Trustee, your body, shape, and form. That's why Poppy took the precaution to make you Herman Q. Louse. He was hedging his bets. Whomever has the code of Herman Q. Louse when Poppy dies automatically ascends to the position of Executive Controlling Partner and in our plot, the key to the Controller's office."

"Then it had nothing to do with Poppy's fantasy?"

"No, nothing at all, really. Only that Barnum and Sherwood believed it. But really it was just so when you walked into the Controller's office it was you transferring what was yours to a bank on the tropical island of Z."

"But really, you transferring what was yours."

"Yes, in a manner of speaking."

"So you couldn't get to what they knew you wanted without me."

"I think you've got it."

"But what reason would you have for escaping without the money?"

"Theoretically, no reason at all."

"And that's why I became you and you became Mr. Moorcraft and Mortimer Blank became the figure of ridicule."

"Yes."

"So you're taking the money," I confirm.

"That's my intention."

"All of the money?"

"Most of it," he says, nodding his head. "I have no choice in the matter. Either I take the money or I don't take the money."

The mirrors continue throughout the halls, making passageways that appear to turn left and turn right. I have to hold onto the real Herman Q. Louse in order not to falter, in order not to run into mirrors. And I now understand how it is no one could possibly find him.

"I don't want to stay and fight. You have to understand, Mortimer, I'm more like you, you're more like me. I'm taking what Poppy has chosen to give me and fulfilling his wish."

"On the tropical island of Z."

"A beautiful place in the Gulf of R."

"Just tell me one more thing."

"Yes, what is it?"

"What about everyone else?"

"They'll be fine. They'll be free to return to their lives as soon as they regain consciousness."

"It somehow doesn't feel right. We were complicit. We could have defied a little. Done something extraordinary."

"Come now. The arrangements are made, it's time to go."

"It could have come sooner," I assert.

"But it's coming now. Now is the time. It's the best I could do. I'll suffer, Mortimer. I promise, I'll suffer."

"How do you suffer rich on the tropical island of Z.?"

"Just follow me. Follow me."

21. THE FINAL FLIGHT

THE FINAL FL

Herman opens another vault-like door at the end of the hall. I follow after him with my heavy briefcase under my arm. A feeling of light-headedness takes hold of my body as the melody I've been humming all evening returns. I still don't know where it comes from or what it is. It's caught on the roof of my mouth and I realize there are words that go with it. I can see myself in the rear view mirror of a car, singing them as I look back to a dark stretch of highway recessing into the distance beyond my tail lights whose crimson glow matches the color of my tearful eyes. I can feel little deaths occur in my spirit with each passing phrase. I feel as if I have done something wrong, if not horrible; a simple act of cowardice, perhaps, that destroyed me long before I ever arrived in G.

"Now be careful, Mortimer," Herman says to me as he opens a door.

"Yes," I say.

He walks through the threshold and steps into the darkness. As I approach the entry I see there is a ladder leading up and down. Down, I see nothing. It looks like a bottomless pit. Up is Herman climbing to the higher floors.

"Don't be afraid," he calls down. "But come quickly."

I step out onto the ladder and as I take my first step up, the briefcase clumsily slips away from my crooked thumb. I grunt and then grope for it, and as I watch it drop I want to dive after it.

"Let it go," Herman calls down to me. "All that it had to tell you, you'll soon know yourself."

The briefcase drops into the shaft and is swallowed by the darkness. I feel part of myself falling with it as though I have just experienced a minor shock of vertigo. I begin climbing quickly and catch up to Herman, whose body is swiveling about. All I can think of is his great weight falling on top of me and plummeting us down to the basement.

"It isn't much farther, Mortimer," Herman assures me.

We climb toward a dim square of light. With every new rung it grows brighter. When we finally reach the light Herman begins banging at the center of the square. He pushes up on it with his palm and moves it off to the side. The narrow passage becomes illuminated to the point that I'm blind to the rungs. Herman climbs through. I climb after him, cautiously reaching for each thin strip of metal. When I reach the top, Herman takes hold of me and nearly lifts me through.

When my eyes adjust to the brightness, I can now see that I am in Poppy's study. We have come through a stained glass floorboard the same color as the carpeting. I recognize the smell of leather and the stagnant air. The vault full of butterflies is open and I can hear someone inside rummaging about. After a moment, Helga Zimmerwitz leans her head out.

"Oh, hello, Mr. Blank," she says with a smile.

"Hello, Ms. Zimmerwitz," I say.

Helga smiles some more and then turns to Herman. "Do we need to take all of these?"

"No," Herman says. "Only as many as you can fit in the bag."

"O.K.," she says cheerfully, and she pops her head back into the vault.

"You have a decision to make, Mortimer," Mr. Louse says as he replaces the panel on the floor, distracting me from the sight of Ms. Zimmerwitz.

"What is it?" I ask.

Mr. Louse removes the piece of paper he ripped from the pad earlier when he was in Mr. Blackwell's chambers and hands it to me. On it are a number of codes.

"Poppy has planned for you to go to the city of N. and activate these accounts."

"What are they?"

"Retribution payments for injustices done to you and the others."

"I see," I say.

"All you need to do is hand the list over to a Mr. Milken at S. Bank in N. You and the rest of the staff of G. will be properly reimbursed for your time, patience, and hardship. Poppy has assured me."

"He's been very generous," Ms. Zimmerwitz assures as well. Her head is sticking out of the vault again.

"You won't be disappointed, Mortimer," Mr. Louse says.

I look at the list of codes and look at Herman and feel that my patience is wearing thin at the thought of this gesture. I fold up the piece of paper and place it in my pocket.

"If you are willing, then, I will ask you to do one more thing before we leave," he says.

"Yes, what is it?"

"I need you to go to Poppy's chambers and bring him back here."

"What will you do with him?"

"You'll see when you return," he says. "He has planned for all of us. Just go, Herman. We don't have much time."

I consider his request, thinking that there is no reason for me to do anything but walk out the front door.

"I'll be back shortly," I say.

"Mortimer?"

"Yes."

"You'll be away from here soon."

"Yes, Mr. Louse."

I exit the study and walk out into the southern wing along the glass cabinets of paper planes. When I approach the western wing I find all the members of the 6 A.M. cleaning crew face down on the linoleum. When I reach the kitchen, I can see Mr. Lutherford and Mr. Heinrik are still sprawled on top of Ms. Morris. I continue down the dim, silent hall toward Poppy's chambers. I walk through the main entrance to find the lights turned all the way up.

Poppy sleeps soundly. His gaunt face is ashen and sweating. He breathes slowly and laboriously as though his heart and lungs are the only things left of his body that still function. The clothes Ms. Lonesome left out hang over the back of the wheelchair stationed next to the western night table. I step between the wheelchair and the bed and, with my bare hands, take hold of Poppy's wrist and feel for his pulse. It beats once for every two breaths I take. When it does beat, it feels like a small fly buzzing and suffocating under the grip of my fist.

I let go of Poppy and walk to Bathroom Number Three, thinking, What act of courage does it take to destroy someone already so destroyed? I enter the supply closet and pull out a pair of shears from a drawer. I then return to his bedside. I kick some legal pads under the bed, bend over, and pull him close to me, wondering if I have ever cradled death in my arms before, wondering why I treat him with such respect considering his role in all this.

I pick up the shears and rest Poppy's head in my lap. I admire his vulgarity for just a moment, and then take hold of his greasy beard. I pull his chin toward me, and then holding the ends of the beard tight, I cut a large clump of hair. Holding it up to the light, I consider its texture, then throw it onto the bed. I begin cutting it all away in large clumps. I cut and I snip and sculpt around the edges of his jaw, away from his cheeks, under his chin, until the bed and the floor are covered in matted gray hair and Poppy's beard is trimmed, motley as it is, close to his face.

I then carefully lift him up onto his headboard from under his arms and lift my shoe onto the bed as I hold his shoulder with my knee to keep him steady. I take a fistful of the hair spreading around his crown and clip away just over his ears. I pull him forward and cut away at the nape his neck. I cut close to the scalp so that there is only a centimeter or two raised. I cut the few hairs rising off his crown. I then remove my knee, step off the bed, and grab him under his shoulders to lower him back down. I take hold of his pinkie between my thumb and forefinger and snip away the curling nails of his hands. Each nail flips into the air and lands in the mulch at my feet. When I'm finally done I look up to find Ms. Lonesome, glowing in the bright light like an apparition, standing beside his wheelchair.

She holds out his clothes for me.

"Hello, Mr. Blank," she says.

"Hello, Ms. Lonesome," I say.

"It's a fine morning," she says.

"Yes it is," I say. "I hope the day is equally as fine."

I look at her. She looks away from me. And I take the clothes from her hands without saying another word. I lay them down in a pile beside Poppy's head. I carefully pull his limp body around so that his legs hang off the edge of the bed. Struggling with the flimsiness of his limbs, Ms. Lonesome and I slip on his pants. I pull his upper torso toward me by his shoulders and Ms. Lonesome lays out the shirt on the bed. I ease him down onto it and gently slip his arms into the sleeves. I button the buttons down his chest and his cuffs. I tuck the front tails into his pants. I turn him over and Ms. Lonesome tucks in the back tail. I turn him over again and clasp the clasp at his waist. Zipper the fly. Ms. Lonesome rolls on his socks. I stick his feet into his shoes and tie up the laces.

"We'd better hurry, Mortimer," she says.

"Yes, Ms. Lonesome," I say, looking at her with wonder.

In the same manner that I put on his shirt, I put on his jacket. I adjust the sleeves. I straighten his pants. We lift him up into the wheelchair so that he is sitting upright. We place his shoes on the stirrups. We step back and look at our handiwork. Ms. Lonesome bends forward and brushes away whatever hair and whatever flakes of skin have clung to his clothes. For the first time since I have known him, he looks like a man.

With one hand on his shoulder and the other on the handle of the chair, I push him around the bed to the door and out into the hall. Poppy's head hangs low, but Ms. Lonesome, with a hand on his shoulder, manages to keep him erect. I am no longer nervous or ambivalent, especially with Ms. Lonesome by my side, walking as she does, being who she is. Her motions eradicate whatever doubt I could ever feel about myself. For the first time I can remember, I actually feel like a man.

"Let whatever may come come, Ms. Lonesome."

"Yes, Mr. Blank," she says, clomping in her heels, stepping over the arms and legs of the cleaning crew that have begun to writhe a little with life.

We weave around all the groggy bodies until we turn the corner of the southern wing. We move fast, so fast the planes in the cabinets look as though they are hovering in flight. One after the other, they blur by me.

When we arrive at the study door, I knock.

"Mr. Louse!" I call out. "Mr. Louse!"

The door opens.

Helga Zimmerwitz stands before us dressed in a flight jacket and ascot.

"Good morning, Ms. Lonesome," she says, and then nods at me.

"Ms. Zimmerwitz," we say.

She is bubbly and buxom.

"Nice to see you again."

Herman is off to the side near the desk carrying a large sack over his shoulder. "Come this way," he says, now looking at Poppy dressed and groomed. "That's very nice," he remarks as he leads us into the back of the study. We walk into a dimly lit room I have never been in.

"What are you planning to do with him?" I ask as Herman pulls open a large cabinet to reveal an elevator door.

"We're going to take him on his final flight. And drop you at your destination."

"And how do you propose to do that?"

"You'll see," he says.

Herman presses the button of the elevator.

The doors open, we enter and ride up.

When the elevator doors open I find that we have been let out onto the roof. The sky is so bright that I can hardly stand it. As my eyes adjust I breathe the fresh hot air of the wind. It whistles into my ear in such a way that I suddenly have the image of myself walking through the silt of the desert. I can feel it clinging to my eyebrows and my fists.

I follow Mr. Louse out onto the vastness of the roof. It stretches out so far I can hardly see its edge. All I can see is a runway that leads back to a replica of the German Gotha flown by Roy Ruteledge at the end of *H.A. 13-3*. In the distance the incomplete silver dome of Paradise rises into the sky. It reflects the sun so brightly I can't stand to look at it for more than a moment.

I follow Mr. Louse's immense shadow as we walk over to the plane. Ms. Lonesome walks by my side, silent and aloof; she seems rigid compared to Ms. Zimmerwitz's bounciness. I wonder what it is about Helga that Herman finds interesting. Just as I think this, Herman turns to Helga and they look at each other as though they have finally come to the point in the plot in which they should gaze knowingly into each other's eyes. There is a brightness in Herman's cheeks as Helga lays her hand on his belly and stands on her toes to kiss his flushed face and whisper something in his ear.

"Here, help me get him up, Mortimer," Herman says, turning away from Helga.

Herman lifts Poppy from the wheelchair and rests him against his chest. I climb up into the cargo hold of the plane. Herman hands Poppy to me. I gently grab him under his arms and pull him up. I cradle him against my chest and walk him through the short narrow space to the tiny cockpit door. Knowing he isn't feeling a thing, I stick his legs through, then station his body into the copilot seat. I fasten his seat belt and strap on his shoulder harness. Ms. Zimmerwitz pulls the sack up from Herman and pulls it toward the cockpit. She begins unloading the glass cases of butterflies and lays them out onto Poppy's lap and then takes a seat in the cargo hold, to the left of the cockpit. She straps herself in and smiles at me. Ms. Lonesome then gets aboard, followed by Mr. Louse, who has moved the wheelchair off to the side.

"Those are for you," he says to me and looks at Ms. Lonesome. He points at two parachutes crowding the corners of the cargo hold. "Let me show you," he says.

"Is this necessary?" I ask as Ms. Lonesome slips her arms through one parachute's straps.

"Yes, Mortimer. You'll enjoy it. Trust me."

"I'll show you, Mortimer," Ms. Lonesome says. "Arms and legs," she says. "Just like so." Ms. Lonesome points to what she has done. And I do it, too. I pull the heavy pack toward me. Herman lifts it up and rests it on my back. Ms. Lonesome secures the straps and the harness. There is a lot of clicking and pulling and the next thing I know I am all strapped in with the round metal handle of the rip cord hanging from my chest.

"Leave the hull door open," he says, looking at me. "I'll tell you when."

In a way I already know. I have been watching it done for some time now. I have no fear. I want to do this. I want to jump to earth. Oh, what a relief it will be when I finally get there, to the ground, to feel the ground.

"There is a car waiting for you," he says. "Take it onto the highway and go east, in the direction of N. No one will find you. I've given you what you need."

I look at Ms. Lonesome and then back to Mr. Louse and then at Helga Zimmerwitz, who is so full of smiles I can't help but find her endearing.

Herman, barely able to climb through the cockpit door, takes his seat next to his father and turns on the engines. The explosion of propeller wind erupts through the chambers. I can already feel my body descending through the air and we haven't even moved yet. I want to feel motion again. I want to float and fall one last time and feel myself sink into the grit of the earth. For a moment I have a sensation of that briefcase falling through the shaft of darkness into the bowels of the building underneath us and I wonder what it might have revealed.

"In time you'll have everything back," Helga says as she sticks a piece of gum in her mouth and jabs her finger at her temple. "Hermee got me kicked already. I remember everything." She laughs. "Have I gotta story, boy." Helga smacks her gum. Ms. Lonesome ignores her and looks out into the sky. For the first time since I have faced her I can see lines forming around her eyes, as though the sunlight has instantaneously aged her.

Ms. Lonesome turns her point of view from the sky to me, looks closely, observes my face. I don't look away from her. I want to fall to earth with you, I think. I want to fall to earth with you.

"I want to fall to earth with you," I say.

The engines wind up and the plane begins to move as Celia turns away from me and looks back to the blue sky. We both take hold of a strap overhead and hold firm as Herman accelerates down the runway. The motion of the plane rises in my throat as the wind rushes into the hull and wraps itself around my cheeks with heavy thrusts. I can feel every motion the plane takes as it lifts and falls and lifts off the roof. I look to the cockpit where I can see Herman's arms maneuvering the plane and I notice Poppy's head turning in search of the view. He is cradling a box of butterflies in his palms.

The plane dips and turns and straightens as we lift off. When we clear the building I can feel the pull of gravity on the nose. We pass the hills I was looking at last night in Mr. Sherwood's office. I can see men milling about, trucks crawling toward the immense silver starfish-of-a-building. I can see the deep craters from the explosions where part of the structure has yet to be started and have a vision of what Poppy's chambers would have looked like, finished, shrouded in bright constellations. And I have an image in my mind of the structure, many years from now, very slowly deteriorating in the arid climate.

As we lift higher into the air, we circle the skyscraper for a second time. It reflects the sun in every window facing east.

"There they go, Mr. Blank," Herman screams back at me.

Helga yelps with glee. "Look at them!" she screams and giggles.

A large group of men and women in gray flannel suits have wandered outside the building. Some are traipsing through the parking lot. Others huddle in small groups. They point up to us, using their hands and arms to shield their eyes from the sun.

Herman turns on a stereo that amplifies Mozart's "Requiem" through the hull, with a dull, pulsing rhythm keeping time with the drone of the engines. The music undulates through my head and I hear the melody that was following me all night, and for whatever reason I now recall the song I've been trying to remember…

Time after time / I tell myself that I'm / So lucky to be loving you / So lucky to be / The one you run to see / In the evening when the day is through.

I can't place where it's coming from, but I remember the stereo in the room and the voice coming from behind. I can hear her voice…as I drive in the car down the dark road behind the truck.

I only know what I know / The passing years will show / You've kept my love so young, so new / And time after time / You'll hear me say that I'm / So lucky to be loving you.

We fly into the distance away from the rising sun and sit listening to Poppy's music, silent as we ride through the bumpy stream of air.

"Are you ready, Ms. Lonesome?" Mr. Louse screams over the engines.

"Yes," she says.

I inch over to the open door and look out to the ground and see the metal of the car shimmering back the morning sun. We are some miles away from G. The land is barren, layered with red and orange sediment. I am still focused on the face in my memory. I can see her head from behind, her hair in her face.

Ms. Lonesome crouches at the door of the plane, looking down to the vastness of the desert. I look at her and can see myself reaching out to her face, taking hold of her chin and kissing her on the lips, there shrouded under the starry sky of the cupola in Paradise.

Ms. Lonesome looks at me. And I suddenly have a vision of her sitting before me in a red velvet dress.

"See you on the ground, Mortimer," she says in a barely audible voice. Then without the slightest hesitation, she jumps and is carried off into the wind.

"Follow her, Mortimer," Herman says.

I look into the cockpit for a moment and see Herman looking back at me. Helga is looking at me. I can see Poppy's hand is no longer gripping the butterfly but it is swinging limp at his side. And for some strange reason there is a bird headed directly toward the windshield. The bird's wingspan is long and elegant, and just like Herman it is looking back, maybe for its flock, I think. And then, sure enough, the flock rises behind it, and I think I won't say anything because suddenly I can see that face in my head as we turn toward each other and I can see her singing into the small, closed eyes of a child and I understand what it means and I can feel what's been lost.

"It's time, Mr. Blank," Herman says.

"All right," I say slowly and deliberately.

As the birds are only inches away from the thin windshield, I can see them as clearly as the faces in my head and I can hear the voice singing a little off-key. With the wind rippling my cheeks I don't look to the ground, but I jump as I hear the glass crash and the screams shrill and it all drifts away and I am finally falling.